The Sea Serpent

There was something very strange about Serpenton. It felt lost somehow—as if half of it wasn't really there. As if it was waiting for something . . .

Fourteen-year-old Helena reluctantly goes to spend the summer holidays in Serpenton, a remote seaside village, to help look after seven-year-old Trevor. While there, she becomes involved with the local amateur dramatic company who beg her to play the leading part in a play about a local legend, the sea serpent. Helena is delighted, but soon she begins to notice something odd about the company: the little boxes they all wear slung over their shoulders; their old-fashioned clothes—and, strangest of all, the fact that no one else can see them.

And then she learns about the bomb that landed on the village in the Second World War . . .

FRANKIE CALVERT spent her childhood in Hornchurch, Essex; her teenage years in North Wales, and then came back south to do English and Drama at the West London Institute of Higher Education. After graduating, she wrote and acted with various theatre companies, including being half of a cabaret double-act. She has worked in several West End theatres in the varying roles of usherette, bar-tender, stage-door keeper, and Box Office clerk—all while continuing to write.

The Sea Serpent is Frankie Calvert's first novel for young adults, and her first book for Oxford University Press.

GW00727951

The Sea Serpent

THE
Sea Serpent

Frankie Calvert

Oxford University Press

Oxford New York Toronto

Oxford University Press, Great Clarendon Street, Oxford OX2 6DP

Oxford New York
Athens Auckland Bangkok Bogota Bombay
Buenos Aires Calcutta Cape Town Dar es Salaam Delhi
Florence Hong Kong Istanbul Karachi
Kuala Lumpur Madras Madrid Melbourne
Mexico City Nairobi Paris Singapore
Taipei Tokyo Toronto

and associated companies in
Berlin Ibadan

Oxford is a trade mark of Oxford University Press

Copyright © Frankie Calvert 1997
First published 1997

A CIP catalogue record for this book is available
from the British Library

Cover design by Slatter-Anderson

ISBN 0 19 271739 1

Printed and bound in Great Britain by
Biddles Ltd, Guildford and King's Lynn

CHAPTER ONE

At The Start Of The Summer

'Helena's doing handsprings over the living room chairs,' said one of her brothers treacherously.

Their mother left the runner beans at once and went to see.

'I've told you before!' she cried. 'You'll break something.'

'Are you worried about my limbs or your ornaments?' asked Helena.

There was a pause.

'Don't be cheeky,' said her mother.

Helena sighed and flopped into one of the chairs. She picked up a book from the floor and started reading. It was a play called *The Demon and Mrs Jones*. She wanted to be in it.

'Don't get involved with that,' said her mother. 'Dinner's nearly ready.'

For theatrical effect, Helena tossed the book lightly over her shoulder.

'Helena! That's a library book, isn't it?'

'No.'

'Well, you shouldn't throw books around anyway.'

Helena bit her lip very hard. The usual intense irritation was building up in her and she wanted to fight it. She picked the book up again and kept her eyes down.

Her mother sighed and went back to the beans.

A few minutes later they were all heaping them on to their plates like little green snakes.

Helena looked warily round the table. This was the beginning of the summer holidays which meant that someone would probably start telling her how she ought to be spending them. Someone usually did.

'Well, Helena . . . ' began her mother and her heart sank. 'And what do you plan to do over the—'

Helena suddenly started choking on a chunk of new potato.

The brother she got on the best with banged her on the back very hard. The other one carried on eating. A bee flew in through the window and went straight back out again in alarm.

'Give her some water, quick, quick!' cried her mother, panicking rather.

'That'll make it worse,' said James.

'Then what shall we do?'

But Helena recovered before they had to make the decision. She sat back in her chair, water streaming from her eyes.

'Well,' said Christopher, as if nothing had happened, 'and what *are* you going to do this summer?'

'I want to be in the play,' Helena gasped and wheezed. 'Like last year.'

'The play again?' asked her mother.

'Yes. They're doing *The Demon and Mrs Jones*. I want to be the Demon.'

There was a pause.

'But why don't you do something useful?'

'Who says it isn't useful?'

Another pause.

'Amateur drama societies aren't,' put in Christopher—but still not taking his eyes off his plate.

'They are if you want to be an actress,' said Helena.

This got exactly the reaction she would have expected from two of them: Christopher actually did take his eyes off his pork chop (for a second), raised them disparagingly and went straight back to it. And her mother shifted anxiously and bit her lip. Acting, after all, was so risky.

'But the play was very good last year,' said James unexpectedly.

Helena gave him a grateful glance.

This didn't deter their mother.

'Maybe you could help in an old people's home,' she mused. 'Or look after some children.'

Helena stared at her, speechless with horror.

Two days later, it was Helena's turn for 'supermarket duty'.

Her mother was deciding between tuna in brine or tuna in oil and Helena was at the other end of the section, wrestling with pasta in twists or pasta in butterflies. The shopping trolley was next to her like an ungainly wire beast. Suddenly she heard a voice cry 'Elizabeth!'—and looked down to the other end to see her mother being approached by a younger woman. Helena had met her once before: she was called Christine Melling.

'Hello, Christine!' said Helena's mother.

A little boy in red shorts and a red T-shirt had come up behind them and stopped.

'Hello, Trevor darling!' said Helena's mother.

Trevor belonged to Christine Melling and he was seven years old.

'Hello,' said Trevor. 'I'm very well, you know. I hope you are very well too.'

And he stood, waiting, with his hands behind his back. He didn't fidget and he didn't twitch. He stood as still as a postbox in his red shorts and T-shirt. Helena stared at him, fascinated with horror. What a horrible little boy, she thought. What a slimy little . . . and then her heart sank as deep as the sea when she realized that her own mother and Trevor's mother were saying the names 'Helena' and 'Trevor' quite a lot and seeming to find some sort of connection between them. Mrs Melling also kept saying

3

things like 'little house in Serpenton' and Mrs Woodvine (Helena's mother) looked frequently in Helena's direction and said 'ought to make herself useful' more than once.

The suspense was too much for Helena in the end. She tossed both twists and butterflies into the wire beast and wheeled it towards the tuna fish section. Her mother was still clasping a sample each of 'briny' and 'oily'.

'Where's Serpenton?' said Helena. 'I've never heard of it.'

'Oh no, you wouldn't have!' said Christine Melling gaily. 'It's our very own strange little place that we discovered, isn't it, Trevor?'

'Well, yes,' said Trevor. 'But we didn't really discover it, did we, Mummy? It was Sophie that said we could use her house there in the summer. So Sophie discovered it, not you, Mummy.'

'That will do, Trevor, dear,' said Christine Melling, still smiling sweetly but with a very slight edge to her voice.

Somebody else came up to them then—a man who looked about the same age as Christine. He was wearing a bow tie the same colour as his wife's ear-rings.

'So it's all settled then, is it, Christine?' he said bluffly.

'Er . . . yes, almost, I think, Robin,' said Christine—and she suddenly fixed a great, gushing smile on Helena.

This is it, this is it, thought Helena and braced herself for the worst.

It was her own mother that spoke next, not Trevor's:

'Mr and Mrs Melling have something to suggest to you,' she said.

'We're going to paint, you see!' said Robin impulsively.

Everyone looked at him.

'Oh . . . I mean, we have purchased some easels and brushes and things. We felt the need to get away from it all. You know how you do sometimes?'

4

'And we have found the most fascinating little place by the sea,' continued Christine.

'Sophie invited us because she lives there,' put in Trevor. 'That's how Mummy and Daddy knew about it and—'

'Thank you, Trevor,' said Christine.

Trevor stopped—perfectly placidly. He folded his arms and regarded them all.

Christine suddenly stopped gushing and got down, rather startlingly, to business.

'We intend to spend the summer painting,' she said. 'And our friend, Sophie, has said we can use her house by the sea because she won't be there all summer.'

'She might never come back to it,' said Trevor. 'She doesn't like it. She wishes she'd never gone to live there because she says it's creepy.'

Christine shot a look at her husband.

'Go and look at that interesting packet of washing powder, Trevor,' said Robin.

Trevor obediently moved off and stood with his back to them all, looking at it.

' . . . and we need someone to help look after Trevor for us while we're painting,' said Christine. 'Your mum has told us you're at a bit of a loose end this summer, Helena, dear . . . '

Has she now? thought Helena indignantly. Not true at all.

' . . . so we wondered if you would be interested in coming on holiday with us.'

In an aside to Helena's mother she added, 'Of course, we could come to some arrangement about paying her for helping.'

It seemed to Helena that the whole of her summer was stretching before her with dreary skies and no Drama. Depression would crash in on her.

Trevor, meanwhile, had pulled a plastic flower from the packet of washing powder and come back to present it to Helena's mother.

'This is for you,' he said and stepped back.

'Oh, Trevor!' cried Mrs Woodvine. 'How lovely!'

'But he pulled it off the packet!' cried Helena. 'It was a free gift if you bought the washing powder!'

Trevor smiled engagingly.

'If you come and help look after me, then your mummy and daddy will miss you, won't they?' he said.

'I can't see that my "daddy" will,' said Helena. 'He lives in Scotland.'

'But why—'

'We must finish the shopping, Trevor, darling,' said Christine swiftly.

That night, there was a play that Helena wanted to see on television. At first, it looked as if it was going to be easier than usual. Christopher, who usually made a point of wanting something on another channel, was out; James was absorbed in a book in a corner and their mother was upstairs, 'sorting something out'.

Helena turned the television on and sat back in the red armchair that Christopher usually occupied. Only the lamp was on—not the main light—making the living room more mysterious and cave-like. The television screen glimmered like a magic lantern. Her brain seemed to divide into two parts: one part concentrating on what was in front of her and the other dreaming about the day when she would be on television herself. She became so deeply absorbed in both things that when her mother made a visitation and snapped the main light on, she nearly jumped out of her skin.

'Now, Helena,' said Mrs Woodvine briskly, 'are you going to take that holiday offer?'

'I'm watching this!' she cried indignantly.

'But Christine Melling does need to know, Helena.'

'She doesn't need to know this minute, does she? It can wait till after this finishes!'

'But what time does it finish?'

'Oh, I don't know. Half-past eleven or something.'

'It'll be too late to ring her then.'

Pause.

'Helena . . . '

'I'm watching this!'

Her mother came and sat down in the other armchair.

'What do you think, James?' she asked.

James was always good-tempered—but then he was at the later end of his teens, unlike Helena at the earlier end of hers. He was less under anyone's jurisdiction.

He kept his place in his book with his finger and looked up.

'What do I think about what?' he asked.

'Don't you think going on holiday with the Mellings would do Helena good?'

'Depends what they're like,' he said cautiously. 'What's wrong with her just being in the play if she wants to?'

'And it isn't just "going on holiday",' put in Helena. 'It's helping to look after that kid.'

'Playing with Trevor won't do you any harm!' cried Mrs Woodvine.

'Mum, why would I want to hang around with a seven year old?'

'Well, when I was your age,' began their mother, 'I was looking after all the children in the neighbourhood and I wouldn't have dreamt of spending a whole summer just pleasing myself and being in a play and—'

That did it! Helena leapt up from the chair and turned the television off.

7

'All right!' she cried. 'I'll go to Serpenton. I'll go, I'll go! At least it means not having to see you for a while!'

She felt the usual horror and guilt the moment the words were out of her mouth and fled the communal room to escape to her own.

CHAPTER TWO

Helena Goes To Serpenton

Helena's mother saw her off at the station a week later. The Mellings had gone two days before and Helena was now to join them. She was all set on stepping into an empty compartment but her mother wouldn't let her.

'I'd be happier if I knew you were sitting with other people,' she said.

'But why?' protested Helena. 'I wanted to be alone because I wanted to act *The Demon* out loud.'

The Demon and Mrs Jones was sticking out of her pocket.

'But there's no point now, is there?' said her mother rather tactlessly. 'You're not going to be in it now.'

It was just as well that Helena was prevented from replying: there was a diversion in the shape of James appearing as if from nowhere. Quite odd really. It was not at all like James to rush.

'Oh, Lenna!' he said—and that was odd as well. He hadn't called her 'Lenna' for years. 'I wanted to see you before you went.'

This was just the kind of thing their mother liked—an example of sweet affection between the brothers and sister. It made her look behind her, half expecting to see Christopher as well—but he didn't appear.

Helena was in a carriage now, standing at the window. There were several respectable-looking people occupying the seats around her. Mrs Woodvine was glad of that.

'Goodbye, Lenna,' said James. 'If it gets too bad, why don't you write to me? I'll be—'

'James!' cried his mother, scandalized. 'What do you mean "if it gets too bad"? Christine Melling is a very nice woman and Trevor is a little darling and I think a little holiday by the sea is just what Helena needs and . . .'

'Goodbye,' said Helena faintly. The train was starting to jerk beyond their reach.

'Goodbye!' called her mother and brother.

Helena distinctly saw the former raising a handkerchief to her eye. Well! she thought. She wanted me to 'go and do my duty' more than anyone and now she's crying about it!

As soon as they were out of sight, she walked through a door and entered the empty carriage after all.

The train was passing by a field of cows. Helena gazed at them and wished she was one of them. All day long they chewed and stared and nobody expected them to go and help look after little boys in Serpenton.

Helena opened *The Demon and Mrs Jones* and started being the Demon. Acting out the part, she alternately stood up, sat down and paced up and down for a long time, only stopping when the train did. Then she gave a quick glance at the name of the station, waited for the train to move off again and continued performing.

When it was on the move, the carriage, to Helena, was no longer a carriage. It was a theatre. The British Rail upholstery turned from scratchy blue to plush red velvet. These seats were no longer empty. People were in them, laughing and clapping—and all for her. There were no longer luggage racks above her head—they were gilded plaster cherubs—and the modest light fittings were enormous chandeliers, reaching down like glass octopuses.

After about an hour and a half's travelling, 'SERPENTON' loomed up behind her window and she had to stop, breathe normally again and get out. This might have felt like a real anti-climax but the moment her feet were on the platform, a seagull made a noise overhead that pierced her to the heart. Seagulls seem to do this to some people. This, then, was more sensation and she closed her eyes. How could she have forgotten the pull from the sea? Why had she been so reluctant to come to Serpenton?

And then a voice called from a few feet away, a human voice this time, and she remembered. The seagull had passed on for the moment and the sea-charm had gone with him. The earlier theatrical charm would have to be re-applied later. Helena began to walk slowly towards the ticket barrier where the three members of the Melling family were waiting for her.

'Hello, Helen dear!' cried Christine Melling.

'Helena,' said Helena at once, thinking she might as well get it over with.

'I beg your pardon?'

'My name's Helena, not Helen. Helena with an "a" on the end.'

She felt very weary when she said it. It was something she had had to do with a lot of people over the years.

'I see,' said Christine Melling. 'Well, I'm sorry to hear you object to the name Helen seeing as it was my mother's name.' And she smiled rather faintly and tragically.

Helena sighed.

'It isn't that I object to it,' she said. 'It's just that it isn't my name.'

'Very well then. And please feel you can call me Christine and not Mrs Melling or anything formal like that.'

'All right then, Christina,' said Helena deliberately.

'Christine,' said Mrs Melling at once. 'Not Christina . . . ' and then she realized how neatly she had fallen into the trap and didn't look tragic any more—just annoyed.

At this point, her husband saw fit to speak:

'Yes, yes, funny business about names, isn't it?' he said, picking up Helena's suitcase and trying to usher them all in the direction of the waiting car. 'People used to call me Robert instead of Robin. Most annoying! But what about you, Trevor? You're quite satisfied that people get your name right, are you? Ha, ha!'

'Yes, Daddy,' said Trevor demurely and stepped into the car.

It had not been a good start. I shouldn't have been rude to Mrs Melling, Helena thought miserably. Not so soon. Another seagull started calling overhead again which was a real relief. Then it was joined by several others.

Just as they were approaching the car, a woman with a walking stick came marching briskly up to the station. Evidently, the walking stick was not because she was lame but because she just chose to walk with it. It seemed to Helena that this person was going to bump right into her so she leapt nimbly on to a low wall to avoid being flattened. *The Demon and Mrs Jones* fell out of her pocket and landed at the woman's feet. The woman looked at her then—and such an expression of amazement came over her face that Helena was alarmed.

'Is . . . is anything wrong?' she asked the stranger.

The stranger seemed to have trouble breathing for a few seconds.

'Is anything wrong?' repeated Helena.

The woman didn't say anything at first—but stooped to pick up the book at her feet.

'What's this?' she said then and looked at it.

Everything seemed to go completely silent and still for a moment. The seagulls stopped shouting. Nobody moved.

Then:

'Are you fond of The Drama?' asked the woman in an odd, laboured voice.

'Oh yes!' said Helena.

'Never thinks of anything else her mother says,' said Robin, hovering around.

'Really?' said the woman.

Then the seagulls started calling again so loudly that everyone looked up, startled, to the sky. Everyone, that is, except for the woman. She was still looking penetratingly at Helena. Helena started to feel dizzy.

'Daddy!' called Trevor from the open door of the waiting car. 'I'll miss my television programme!'

The woman turned her head—and Helena felt as if she had been released from something.

'Coming, Trevor!' Robin called back. 'Nice talking to you,' he said to the woman. 'We must go now.'

'Goodbye,' said Helena and put *The Demon and Mrs Jones* in her pocket.

'Goodbye,' said the woman—and then added 'for now' in a softer voice. She looked at Helena as the car was moving off—and Helena saw her do it because she was looking through the back window at the time.

'Who was that?' she asked Robin and Christine—and found that she was quite shaky.

'No idea,' said Robin. 'We haven't got to know anyone in Serpenton yet.'

'She was a bit odd, wasn't she?'

'Was she? She probably just isn't used to dealing with young people. You never see any here, you know. It's extraordinary.'

This depressed Helena rather a lot. She stole a glance at Trevor sitting on the back seat next to her. He was very composed with his hands neatly folded on his knees. He kept his eyes straight ahead and didn't move.

There was something very strange about Serpenton. You could sense it even through the windows of a car. It felt lost somehow—as if half of it wasn't really there. Helena rubbed her eyes, wondering if there was something wrong with them. The little grey houses seemed to be coming and going as if a fog were drifting in front of them—and then not. But it couldn't be foggy—not in the middle of the summer. Could it? Helena wound the window down and tried to understand exactly what was happening—or not happening. But she couldn't.

The car was running slowly along a road on the one side of which was a row of houses and a small pub. The pub was called 'The Sea Serpent'.

'I've never come across a pub called that before,' said Helena—and looked at the sign that was swinging from it. There could have been a whirly sort of amphibian painted on it but it was too faded to see properly. Then something made her look to the other side of the road and she saw the sea.

Her heart gave a lurch.

'Please,' she said. 'Can we just stop and run down to the sea?'

'Run down to the sea?' said Robin. 'Before tea, you mean?'

'Yes,' said Helena. 'If you don't mind.'

The sea wasn't in a particularly good mood. It was sulky and mottled green. Helena had the idea it was very full of seaweed at the moment.

'Maybe just a quick paddle if you insist,' said Christine. 'But you mustn't be long. Trevor wants to see *Science For Children* at four o'clock, don't you, Trevor?'

'That's right,' said Trevor. 'It's a programme on television, you know. It's not as good as *Tomorrow's World* but that's for grown-ups, isn't it, Mummy? I can watch that when I'm older, can't I, Daddy?'

'Yes, darling,' said Robin and Christine together.

Nobody but Helena wanted to walk on the beach. I suppose they've been doing it every day, she thought.

The sand wasn't any less moody than the sea was. It was damp and gritty. But at the same time it made Helena want to walk and walk on it—like getting to know a slightly mysterious person. She went straight to the water, bent down and put her hand in it. A twist of green seaweed floated over her fingers like a snake. With the wet hand all charmed over with salt, she straightened again but there was a great, wild calling of seagulls overhead that made her dizzy—and she suddenly found herself on her knees.

She was a bit frightened by this. There's something weird about this place, she thought. What have I come to?

Then Robin Melling broke the spell.

'Time, time!' he started yelling and she turned round to look at him. Some of the seagulls stopped calling. She made her way back to the car, feeling as if she had been to a seance which had finished too soon because of someone not taking it seriously.

'Little boys go on beaches too,' Trevor remarked when she got into the car. 'But not in the evening.'

They reached the cottage only just in time for *Science For Children*. Trevor put himself in an armchair in front of it and didn't stir for half an hour.

'Come along, Helena,' said Christine Melling. 'Come and make some sandwiches while I put the kettle on.'

'But I thought—' began Helena but halted, biting her lip.

'What did you think?' said Christine.

'I just . . . '

'Well?'

Oh, how I wish I hadn't begun that sentence, thought Helena, but it was too late. She had started and she would have to finish.

'I thought I was here to help look after Trevor, not . . . er . . . not make sandwiches, although I don't mind of course if you're very busy and—'

'As you can see,' said Christine, 'Trevor is watching *Science For Children* like a little lamb and doesn't need any particular attention from you just at present.' And she laughed cheerfully.

'That's right,' said Trevor, without taking his eyes away from the screen. 'Nannies do make sandwiches, you know. They do that as well as looking after little boys.'

'Nannies!' cried Helena in horror. 'I'm not here to be your nanny!'

Trevor smiled and watched intently while a woman on the television was picking up pins with a magnet.

'I said I'm not here to be your—'

'The tuna fish is in the cupboard,' said Christine swiftly, 'and the mayonnaise is in the fridge.'

After Trevor was put to bed, Robin and Christine decided that they ought to go out for half an hour's painting.

'We'll sit on the rocks, you know,' said Robin, 'and paint the sun beginning to drop over the sea.'

'But I thought—' began Helena and then realized she was about to say something else that she probably shouldn't. She went bright red.

'Well, what is it this time?' said Christine.

'Nothing, nothing at all,' said Helena. Just to show that she really meant nothing at all, she marched purposefully to the kitchen sink and started wielding the washing-up liquid.

'Very well then,' said Christine. 'As Robin says, we'll only be about an hour.'

And the two of them swept through the front door, making a great show of their easels and paint brushes.

Left in front of the sink, Helena said what she had meant to say before they left. She said it to the bubbles on the tuna-stained plates:

'I thought I could go out this evening—not just be stuck baby-sitting Trevor. I was going to go back to the sea and now I can't.'

She went at the washing-up a bit fiercely after that. Nothing broke though—it was as if all the crockery turned to rubber because it knew her mood and didn't want to get her into trouble.

She finished the washing-up and decided that she was not going to do the drying-up. She left the slippery plates all frothing at each other on the rack and went back into the sitting room.

Thinking about the strange atmosphere that Serpenton gave off, she remembered what Trevor had said in the supermarket about his parents' friend, Sophie, who owned the cottage they were staying in. According to him, she regretted coming to live in Serpenton because she thought it was creepy. Yes, said Helena to herself, she was right, it is creepy. The woman with the walking stick was exceedingly so. And the seagulls were poised all the time, waiting to cry out about something—but it seemed more definite than seagulls usually were.

A shivering excitement started to creep over her.

She tried to concentrate on *The Demon and Mrs Jones*—but couldn't. This surprised her; it wasn't often that she couldn't draw on a theatrical fantasy to get her through something.

She was pacing up and down when the Mellings came in again. She turned towards them in relief, hoping for normalish conversation. They hadn't been out for very long. They came in through the front door looking rather deflated, Helena thought.

'Didn't you have a good painting session?' she asked them. 'Can I see what you did?'

Robin propped his easel against the wall and sat down.

'Can I see what you did?' said Helena again.

He looked at her.

'Oh . . . er . . . there was too much wind,' he said.

'We thought it wouldn't do to get our paints and things all whipped about,' said Christine.

There was a pause.

'What did you do instead?' asked Helena, prepared to feel very jealous if they had been walking by the sea.

But they hadn't.

'We had a drink,' said Robin. 'In The Sea Serpent. You noticed it today, didn't you? Tiny little place in the road opposite the sea.'

'Funny name for a pub, isn't it?' said Christine—and there was actually a slight sneering in her tone. 'There were three old men in there and that was all. What a pity there isn't more life in this place!'

Helena looked at her in surprise. Up until now, she had only heard them enthusing and boasting about how small and strange and therefore fascinating the place was.

Robin also noticed that his wife's cover was slipping.

'Well, it's not a resort, darling, is it?' he said. 'We don't like resorts, do we? Everyone goes to resorts but we aren't like other people, are we?'

'Oh no, no, of course not!' said Christine hurriedly. 'All I'm saying is, that if it only had a couple of—'

'We're going to paint some lovely pictures, aren't we?' said Robin.

Helena kept her head down and pretended to be taking something out of her pocket because there was a massive smirk on her face which she couldn't do anything about.

'And it was very kind of Sophie to—'

'Oh yes, Sophie,' said Helena, raising her head again, the smirk disappearing because she was interested. 'What was it Trevor said about Sophie finding it creepy? Why did she think it was creepy?'

'Oh, she was just being silly,' said Christine—and went into the kitchen to put the kettle on.

'There was some story she heard from someone in the village,' said Robin vaguely. 'Or half heard. Maybe not even as much as half. Something about a stray bomb that landed here near the end of the war. Why she should find that creepy a whole fifty years later, I have no idea!'

He laughed indulgently.

But Helena didn't feel like laughing. A faintness had come over her which she was not familiar with. She sat down.

'Helena dear!' called Christine from the kitchen—as if she could see through the wall. 'Would you mind just grabbing a tea towel and drying up those plates?'

Yes, I would mind, thought Helena. I would mind very much indeed.

'Haven't they all drip-dried then?' she shouted back. 'I left them so that they could.'

'I'm not sure at all,' said Christine doubtfully.

Well, just pick one up and see if it drips, thought Helena in exasperation.

She waited.

Christine waited.

'Are you coming then?' asked Christine.

'Well, do they drip or not?' Helena almost screamed. Just like my mum, she thought. She's just like her. And I thought I was getting away from all that!

There was an offended silence and Helena knew it was 'offended', not just 'silence'. She sighed and got to her feet. She went into the kitchen and plucked a dish from the drying rack.

'Bone dry,' she said.

'Well . . . could you put them away then?' said Christine, determined that Helena was to do something.

19

CHAPTER THREE

The Sun Not So Bright

The sun was quite dulled the next morning, which suited Serpenton very well. It truly brought out the melancholy and strangeness of the place.

'I don't like it,' said Trevor, holding very tightly to Helena's hand.

'Don't like what?'

'The weather. It's supposed to be hot at the seaside.'

'But it isn't cold, Trevor.'

'I don't want it just not to be cold. I want it to be hot. I want the sun to be all proper and bright yellow.'

No doubt he would have liked the sand to be all proper and bright yellow as well—but it wasn't. Neither was it gritty and moody like the evening before. Today, Helena looked at it and felt rather bored. There seemed to be so much of it—going on and on because the tide was well out. She couldn't see the white glimmer of a single shell to break the monotony—there didn't even seem to be any snakings of seaweed today. It was just grey, grey, grey and stretched, stretched, stretched. She wondered if this was anything to do with the prospect of spending a day with Trevor. Maybe shells and seaweed miraculously appeared when the company was more interesting or if you were just on your own and wanting to walk—like last night.

Over to the left was a very long rocky arm which, although it was very grey too, might well have contained rock pools and neat little beasties living in shells. Helena felt a dawning of hope and was about to suggest to Trevor that they go there when he said, 'Did you bring the mats?'

'What mats?'

'The mats to sit on.'

'We don't need mats, do we? Why don't we go on to the rocks over there?'

'Little boys don't sit on rocks at the seaside. They sit on mats on the sand. We'll have to go back to the cottage and get them, won't we?'

Helena stared at him speechlessly.

'Come on then,' he said and started walking back.

They returned with the mats and laid them on the sand. Trevor put his sweatshirt on and sat down. He carefully set his blue plastic lunch-box on the ground next to him and then folded his hands in his lap.

Oh well, thought Helena, if that's all he wants to do—and she pulled *The Demon and Mrs Jones* out of her pocket and started reading.

'What are you doing?' asked Trevor at once.

'Turning into a demon,' said Helena.

'Well, you mustn't. You're supposed to be playing with me.'

Helena snapped her book shut and very nearly threw it at him—but gained control just in time. She tried very hard to make her voice sound low and kind.

'Well, why don't we make a sand-castle?' she said. 'We could put a moat round it and find some crabs to swim in it and—'

'Find some crabs to swim in the castle?' said Trevor doubtfully.

'No!' Helena cried, exasperated. 'The crabs swim in the moat, not the castle.'

'But do crabs actually swim? I thought they—'

'Do you want to build a sand-castle or not?'

'Not.'

Helena swallowed. She stared at *The Demon and Mrs Jones* lying upside down in front of her. Again, a great sense of stretched-out waiting came over her. The whole of Serpenton waiting for something. Today, on the beach, it felt like a tedious wait; last night it was different—sulky and ruffled. Her hand brushed the cover of *The Demon and Mrs Jones*.

'Don't you start reading that book again,' said Trevor. 'You should be doing things with me—but not sand-castles. I don't like sand-castles. You've got to think of something else.'

Helena very carefully turned her book the right way up. Then she spoke again with the 'low, kind' voice:

'Why don't we go and see what we can find in the rock pools?'

Trevor put his head on one side.

'Hmm,' he said. 'Is that a nice thing to do?'

'Yes,' said Helena.

'Do little boys like doing it?'

The low, kind voice got higher and shriller.

'Yes,' she said. 'And, actually, Trevor, they like making sand-castles too.'

'No, they don't,' said Trevor. 'It's the mummies and daddies that like doing that and then they pretend they've done it for the little boys.'

There was a pause.

'Well, do you want to look for creatures in the rock pools or don't you?' said Helena, dimly aware that she had said something else like this only a few minutes ago.

'Well, we can't really, can we?' said Trevor.

'Why can't we?'

'Because we haven't got any buckets.'

'What do we want buckets for?'

'To put our things in.'

'What things?'

'Our things that we get from the rock pools.'

'But we don't have to put them in buckets.'

'Yes, we do.'

'No, we don't.'

'Yes, we do.'

'No, we don't.'

'Yes, we do, so let's go and buy some.'

'What?'

'Come on.'

'What do you mean "come on"?'

'We've got to buy some buckets.' And he got up, rolled his mat into a neat sausage and tied it with a piece of hairy string he extracted from his pocket. He put it under his arm, picked up his blue plastic lunch-box with the other hand and looked at Helena. For the second time that morning, she found herself being led away.

What Trevor had in mind was the sort of thing he had seen at the seaside before—brightly-coloured buckets with spades to match. But there was nowhere in Serpenton which sold anything like that. Indeed, they hadn't found any shops at all yet.

'I don't understand,' Trevor kept saying. 'This is supposed to be the seaside. They always have buckets and spades at the seaside so why haven't they got them here?'

Helena didn't answer. The streets of Serpenton were very narrow and she looked at the little grey houses with interest. They still seemed lost and waiting for something. That probably didn't change. She could almost have sworn she heard one of them sigh—though it was more likely to be someone inside it, of course.

'Oh look, here's a shop,' said Trevor. 'Let's try in here,'—and he pulled her into a little place that didn't seem to sell anything in particular. There was a counter piled high with chocolate facing you as you went in. In a corner were things like garden forks and flower pots. Very close to the door was

23

a lop-sided pile of dish-cloths. Other things were arranged in fits and starts around the walls and on shelves. The shop was like the rest of Serpenton—drifting and only half there.

'Can I help you?' asked an elderly woman. She was sitting behind the counter of chocolate.

'Yes, you can,' said Trevor at once and strode towards her. 'I want a bucket and spade. The bucket must be royal blue but it doesn't matter what colour the spade is.'

'I think it must have been your parents that came in yesterday,' said the woman. 'I hadn't got what they wanted either.'

'Do you mean you haven't got buckets and spades?' said Trevor indignantly.

'No, dear,' said the woman. 'Not the sort you mean.'

'What did my mummy and daddy want?' said Trevor and then, before she could open her mouth, 'Oh I know, it must have been paintbrushes and things. They do a lot of painting, you know. They're called Robin and Christine Melling and I'm Trevor Melling and this girl has come to play with me and she's called Helen Woodvine.'

'Helena,' said Helena between her teeth. 'Not Helen— Helena.'

'Helen Nah,' repeated Trevor with sarcastic exaggeration. 'Helen Nah.'

Before Helena could deal with this, the woman behind the counter came in smoothly with, 'I'm very pleased to meet you, Helena,' and she pronounced the name exactly right.

'And are you pleased to meet me too?' asked Trevor.

'Oh yes, dear,' said the woman—but she winked at Helena.

Helena decided that she liked this woman very much.

'You'd better buy me some chocolate, Helen Nah,' said Trevor loftily, 'and then we'll go and find a shop where they do sell buckets and spades.'

24

'Then you will be searching for a long time, young man,' said another voice from just behind them.

Trevor turned round to stare indignantly at the woman who had just come into the shop. Helena looked at her too—and recognized her immediately. She was the woman with the stick who was walking to the station yesterday when Helena had just arrived in Serpenton.

'Hello,' she said to Helena.

'Hello,' said Helena uncertainly. She felt the stranger's eyes travel down to her jacket pocket and stare at the book sticking out of it.

'Is it still *The Demon and Mrs Jones*?' she asked.

'Er . . . yes,' said Helena.

'Are you going to buy me any chocolate or not, Helen Nah,' said Trevor.

'Not,' said Helena, without looking at him.

'I really think you better had, you know,' he said.

The woman with the walking stick just turned round and looked at him. He blinked and looked confused for the first time since Helena had known him.

'Why don't you go and count how many different types of chocolate there are?' said the woman—and the tone of her voice made Helena stare at her in surprise. It was completely blank—as if she were putting no real thought into the words and yet her eyes were boring right into Trevor with an intensity that was startling.

Helena turned to Trevor then, curious to see what his reaction would be. She would normally expect him to say something like, 'Oh well, I can't do that, you see, because . . . ' But he didn't. He walked straight over to the counter and started looking at the chocolate.

'That's right,' said the woman with the walking stick. 'There's red wrappers and blue wrappers and gold ones . . . '

There was something very compelling about this: Helena

found her own eyes being drawn towards the colours on the sloping counter. She might even have walked towards them herself—but the woman suddenly cut through her own spell.

'Do you only like reading plays or do you like being in them as well?' she asked Helena. Her mood had changed yet again: this time, she sounded rather defensive.

'I like being in them,' said Helena. 'More than anything else in the world.'

There was an uncomfortable pause.

'May I ask how old you are?' asked her inquisitor.

Helena found herself answering even though she didn't really want to.

'Fourteen,' she said.

The woman stiffened. For a second, her look could only be described as hostile.

Helena wished there was a chair she could sink down on—she felt slightly dizzy—like she had on the beach last night, then again in the cottage. Was she becoming delicate or something? How awful!

'And your name?' asked the woman.

'Why do you want to know that?' said Helena with a sudden rush of renewed vigour. The dizziness passed. After all, why should she just hand out her identity to any stranger that came asking?

'I apologize,' said the woman stiffly. 'I should probably give you mine first.'

Helena said nothing.

'My name is Blaze—Monica Blaze,' she said, and, unexpectedly, held out her hand.

'Mine is Helena Woodvine,' said Helena very quietly. Tentatively, they shook hands.

There was an embarrassed silence. She's worse than my mum, thought Helena.

Then the woman behind the counter spoke. This was a relief. Helena found her much easier to like than the other one.

'Can I serve you with anything, Miss Blaze?' she said comfortably as if she hadn't noticed anything awkward going on. Miss Monica Blaze became brisk and businesslike at once.

'Yes please, Mrs Fields, I want a pound of chocolate brazils and two dishcloths.'

Helena blinked and felt everything come back to normal again—or as normal as anything could be in this place. She looked at Trevor and remembered they had come about a bucket. There wasn't one—and now it was time to go.

'Trevor,' she said firmly, 'we won't get a bucket anywhere here. We'll have to go and look at the rock pools without one.'

'Oh no!' Trevor began to protest. 'I won't look for things in the rock pools without a royal blue bucket.'

'Yes, you will,' said Helena and took him from the shop. She dragged him, screaming, all the way back to the beach.

'I wanted a royal blue bucket!' he bawled. 'A royal blue bucket to put pool-creatures in!'

Helena stood still. She remembered how Monica Blaze had dealt with him and tried to do the same. She stared at him piercingly and made her voice go blank.

'You'll just have to observe them in their natural habitat,' she droned, not caring whether he understood the big words or not.

But Monica's methods didn't work for her.

'Why are you talking in that funny voice?' said Trevor—and then continued to scream. Soon, he had screamed so much that he was sick.

'That's my breakfast,' he said grimly. 'I've put my breakfast all over the sand.'

'Yes, you have, haven't you, dear?' said Helena equally grimly.

'You know what you have to do now, don't you?' said Trevor.

'What?'

'Little boys who are sick on beaches have to be taken home and tucked up in bed. That's what you have to do because you're older than me and you're Helping To Look After Me.'

Helena stared at him, not knowing whether he meant it or not.

And Trevor folded his arms and said, 'I'm waiting.'

Stifling a curse, she grabbed him by the wrist again and took him back to the cottage.

Once he was lying under the bedclothes and his room was suitably darkened, Helena took refuge on the sofa in the sitting room.

She was now going to be stuck indoors all day instead of being by the rock pools which was what she had really wanted to do. She had wanted to slither about and see what was there—and then sit down and imagine she was acting in *The Demon and Mrs Jones* while the sea rolled in front of her like a lively audience. Trevor, of course, would have found some absorbing pursuit of his own by then. Instead, she was, condemned to sit on a scratchy sofa and she found that even with Trevor in bed, she was not allowed to concentrate on her play.

'Helen Nah!' he called imperiously when she had only just opened the book. 'Do you think I ought to have a bucket by my bed in case I'm sick again?'

'I'll be damned if you're going to get a bucket!' shouted Helena furiously. 'It was shouting about buckets that made you sick in the first place!' And she took up a battered old saucepan instead.

'Maybe you should give me a pill,' said Trevor. 'I ought to have a pill because I was sick.'

Helena searched all the cupboards in the bathroom and kitchen but found nothing that looked like a bottle of junior aspirin. In the end, she opened a box of Smarties and presented him with one of the paler ones, balanced on a spoon. He took it and chewed it, quite satisfied.

When Robin and Christine Melling got back after their day's painting, they were rather disconcerted to find that Trevor was already in bed.

'But Trevor doesn't go to bed this early, Helena,' said Christine.

'He wanted to,' said Helena. 'It was his own idea.'

'Yes, because I was sick, Mummy!' called Trevor down the stairs. 'My breakfast came up all over the beach!'

'Oh, darling!' cried Christine and ran upstairs at once.

She came downstairs after a few minutes and, for some reason, she sounded very cheerful.

'Well, Helena!' she said. 'You haven't had to do much today, have you, with Trevor being in bed for most of it!' She laughed merrily. Helena didn't feel in the least like joining in.

'So in that case,' continued Christine, 'you wouldn't mind staying in again tonight with him? It's just that we met some people today. A terribly nice couple, weren't they, Robin?'

'Yes,' said Robin.

'And they asked us to eat with them tonight in a restaurant in Widding. And of course we said we couldn't think of it as you'd been looking after Trevor all day—but as you haven't really been doing that after all, then I'm sure you wouldn't mind staying in again just for tonight. I'm certain it won't happen many more times but, you know, they were such a very nice couple, weren't they, Robin?'

'Yes,' said Robin. 'They were.'

For the second evening running, Helena didn't get to the sea.

CHAPTER FOUR

The Pieman

The next day was much the same except that Trevor didn't throw up. He insisted on chocolate in the afternoon so they went to Mrs Fields's shop again.

'What's the matter, Helena?' asked Mrs Fields, noticing her miserable face. 'Are you sick of our beach already?'

'Oh no!' said Helena. 'I've hardly had a chance to look at it yet.'

'Oh, Helena, don't tell fibs!' spluttered Trevor with his mouth full of chocolate jellies. 'We've been sitting on the beach ever such a lot.'

Helena muttered something about the rock pools.

'I've told you why we can't go to the rock pools,' said Trevor with a kind of adult, heavy patience. 'It's because we haven't got a bucket.'

Helena turned very abruptly and started leafing through the dishcloths. It was either that or hit him.

'Have you been up the High Hat yet?' said Mrs Fields unexpectedly.

'The High Hat?' said Helena. 'What's that?'

'Not heard of our High Hat?' said Mrs Fields in amazement. 'Don't those people tell you anything? The people you're staying with, I mean.'

'My mummy and daddy,' put in Trevor importantly.

'The High Hat is a hill!' cried Mrs Fields. 'Surely you must have seen the hill behind the village?'

'I suppose I must have done,' said Helena—but she wasn't at all sure. It seemed so ridiculous. How could you miss a hill? 'But anyway,' she said, 'let's go and climb it, Trevor.'

'Oh no!' cried Trevor in horror, nearly choking on a chocolate jelly. 'Little boys don't go climbing hills at the seaside. They definitely don't.'

Helena felt rage coming upon her. She opened her mouth to say something but Mrs Fields intervened.

'It's a very interesting hill,' she said. 'We used to have a—' but then she stopped herself.

'What?' demanded Trevor at once. 'What did you use to have?'

'Lots of people going up and down it,' said Mrs Fields smoothly. 'But now they don't.'

The next morning, they were sitting on the sand as usual when something unexpected happened. A pieman walked across the beach. This was the first time they had seen anyone else by the sea at all.

He was a very impressive-looking pieman. He had a great, brown moustache that curled up at each end, and he wore a long, stripy apron and a straw boater hat with ribbon round it. The pies were set out in a tray with steep edges. He had it slung over his shoulder which reminded Helena of an ice cream seller at a theatre. Over his other shoulder, he was carrying something in a canvas case— binoculars or a camera or something. Helena got up and went towards him.

'Helena!' cried Trevor. 'Where are you going?'

'To get you some lunch!' she said over her shoulder.

'What do you mean?' said Trevor, scandalized. 'You're not going to catch crabs or anything, are you? Little boys don't eat crabs for their lunch! I've got my lunch here in my blue box! I don't need anything else!'

Helena ignored this and caught up with the pieman. She had to run because he was going very fast. But now he stopped and looked surprised.

'Hello,' said Helena. 'What sort of pies have you got, please?'

The pieman looked utterly confused.

'Oh . . . er . . . I haven't,' he said. 'I mean, they're not real ones.'

'Not real?'

'No. They're . . . er . . . they're artificial ones.'

'Artificial?'

'Yes,' said the pieman. 'We can't have real ones, you see. You can't get the fats to make the pastry. At least . . . oh well, maybe you can now except that we don't really need real ones, you see, because they're for . . . they're for . . . well, there it is. Good morning to you!' And he started to walk very fast again—as if he had somewhere to get to.

Helena stared after him in amazement. Then she turned round and went back to Trevor. He was sitting bolt upright on his mat and his eyes had been very widely open for some time.

'Helena,' he said in a hushed sort of voice, 'you're going mad! You were talking to yourself for ages! You're not allowed to be mad, you know. If you're going mad, then you won't be able to play with me any more.'

'Don't be stupid, Trevor!' said Helena sharply. 'I was talking to the pieman.'

'What pieman? What is a pieman?'

'Don't mess about, Trevor. He was a very nice pieman except . . . well . . . he didn't have any real pies.'

'Don't be silly, don't be silly, don't be silly!' cried Trevor. He was beginning to work himself into a real tantrum. 'Why are you pretending you saw someone, Helena? I don't like it!'

That evening, Robin and Christine came in looking quite flustered and excited. Helena assumed they were all worked up about their day's painting but after a few minutes she decided they were a bit drunk instead. Robin lay back in an armchair and kept going on about a 'charming little wine bar'. Then he hiccuped and looked terribly embarrassed. Christine explained that they had driven into Widding with their new friends and found a wine bar which looked just the sort of place that artists went to.

'It was research,' she said with her winning smile.

Tomorrow, they were going to go back and paint it because it was so delightful—it had little tables on the pavement and everything.

In the meantime, Robin fell asleep in the armchair and snored very loudly.

'Mummy,' said Trevor in a strange, hard, little voice. 'Helena did something very silly today. She pretended there was a man selling pies on the beach and she talked to him and there was really nothing there at all!'

'That's nice, dear,' said Christine absently.

'You didn't listen, Mummy!' cried Trevor.

Helena couldn't decide who was the oddest; the pieman who didn't have real pies (and she was beginning to wonder whether his moustache was real as well)—or Trevor, who kept insisting he hadn't seen the pieman at all.

CHAPTER FIVE

Two More People On The Beach

The next day, at lunch-time, Helena saved a tiny corner of sandwich and tried another trick to get Trevor to the rock pools.

'Don't you think it would be interesting, Trevor,' she said carefully, 'to leave this bit of sandwich in one of the pools and watch to see if anything comes to eat it?'

'What sort of thing?' said Trevor. 'A seagull or something?'

'Maybe a seagull,' said Helena. 'Or it might be a fishy thing from under a rock or a crab or an anemone or—'

'What a waste of sandwich!' said Trevor. 'Give it to me if you don't want it!' And he snatched the corner of bread from her fingers and stuffed it in his mouth. 'Chocolate now,' he said before he had even finished chewing it—and he stood up, ready to go to Mrs Fields's shop.

But Helena wasn't taking any notice of him. She was looking in the direction of the rock pools because, once again, there were other people on the beach. This time, it wasn't the pieman—it was two girls.

One looked about Helena's age; the other, a little older. They both had brown, wavy hair, held behind their ears with hair combs—and they were wearing flowery, short-sleeved dresses with buttons all the way down the front. Back at home, all Helena's friends were wearing similar things at the moment. Helena herself hadn't managed to persuade her mother to let her have one yet.

'But, darling, they're so dated!' Mrs Woodvine had said.

'How can you say that when everyone's wearing them?' Helena had asked.

'They're like the awful things my sisters wore during the war!'

'And now they're back in fashion. What's wrong with that?'

'But you don't want to be just the same as everyone else, do you?'

'Of course I do!'

Helena knew already that only when you're older can you dare to have an individual style. Even then, it's risky. As a teenager, you have to look the same as all the others or life is hell.

The two girls on the beach were rooting in the rock pools, pretending to push each other over and slithering a little over the seaweed. Helena watched them, thinking how nice it would be to make new friends with people her own age. She had thought that there weren't any in Serpenton. These two were slightly hindered by small, lidded boxes which they each carried on a string over one shoulder and which they kept having to adjust. Helena wondered what was in them. Maybe they were lunch-boxes. Trevor always carried a lunch-box. Trevor spoke then.

'Helena,' he said impatiently, 'what are you looking at? You're supposed to be taking me to the shop!'

Then his face crumbled.

'Oh, you're not pretending about that pieman again, are you?' he whispered. 'You can't! You mustn't!'

'You can see it's not the pieman!' said Helena. 'It's two girls over there by the rock pools. Do you like their dresses?'

'There's nothing there, there's nothing there!' cried Trevor. 'Stop pretending! I don't like it!'

Helena stared at him in surprise and then adopted a gentler tone.

'Trevor,' she said, 'what's the matter? Surely you can see them. They're coming nearer now.'

Trevor shrank away. Deciding the best thing was to ignore him, Helena turned to look at the two girls again.

They were walking slowly in her direction now, chatting to each other. The younger one's shoulder-box kept slipping off and she had to keep hitching it up. The material of her dress got ruffled underneath it.

As they got nearer and she could see what they were wearing more clearly, Helena realized that these dresses were not the nicest she had seen. They were a funny length and the material was odd as well. On their feet they had brown lace-up shoes that looked very old-fashioned. To add to it, the younger one had fawn ankle socks and the older one had brown tights.

They had reached where she was sitting now. They both turned their heads towards her and smiled. A rush of delight went through Helena. As if it mattered what they were wearing! She knew she liked these people and she smiled back. They moved on—and she noticed that the older one's tights had seams up the back which nobody else was wearing at the moment . . . but, again, so what?

The next thing she knew was an indrawn breath behind her—and it didn't sound like Trevor. She could tell it was someone older. She turned round and saw two things. One of them was Trevor running off into the village and the other was Miss Monica Blaze standing quite close behind her and looking as if she had had a great shock.

'Miss Blaze!' said Helena in alarm. 'Are you all right?'

'What? Oh yes . . . yes, thank you,' said Miss Blaze. 'I knew it would be strange seeing them again after all this time but it still . . . well, it still . . . threw me.'

'Seeing who?' said Helena. 'Do you mean those girls? Have they been away then?'

'Yes, yes, they've been away,' snapped Miss Blaze and looked at Helena half with hostility again.

Helena would have felt cross and offended at that, if Monica hadn't sighed—and quite heavily.

'But now they're back,' said Monica. 'And you're here as well.'

She smiled and moved off rather shakily. Her walking stick was coming in for more use than it usually did. She was leaning on it very dependently. It was an interesting stick. It had a sort of scaled pattern on it and the top was carved like the head of a serpent.

Helena, meanwhile, had to go chasing after Trevor in case he fell down and cut his precious little knee or anything like that. She didn't worry about him getting run over; there were never any cars in the streets of Serpenton except the one belonging to his parents and that was safely in Widding.

That evening, Helena politely asked if she could see some of Robin's and Christine's paintings. They both looked very flustered at the request.

'Oh . . . er . . . it might be a bit of a palaver to get all my stuff out now,' said Robin. 'I keep my portfolio very firmly tied, you see and . . . '

'Perhaps tomorrow, dear,' said Christine, smiling sweetly. 'But now I must get Trevor to bed. Look at him drooping all over his dish!'

'I'm not drooping, Mummy!' cried Trevor indignantly and sat up away from his dish at once. There were dark shadows under his eyes.

His mother waggled her finger playfully at him.

'Oh yes, you are!' she fluted and bore him off to bed.

Helena was very surprised. Normally, it was left to her to put Trevor to bed.

CHAPTER SIX

Henry Mead

Trevor still wouldn't agree to doing anything except sitting, but Helena sat on her mat the next morning feeling quite excited. Would there be anyone interesting to see today? The pieman or the two girls or somebody else . . . It almost made up for being put upon with the Trevor business.

The answer was somebody else.

Trevor was sitting as usual with his sweatshirt on, his lunch-box beside him and his hands in his lap. A man in grey flannel trousers and a patterned, sleeveless jumper walked down from the direction of the village and started bending and stooping over the rock pools. Every so often, his hand would dart out like a white fish and he would pick something up.

'Look at that man, Trevor,' said Helena. 'Why don't we go and do that?'

Trevor put his hands over his ears.

'I'm not listening to you,' he said steadily. 'You won't be able to frighten me today because I'm not listening.'

Something went click in Helena's head and she might have been tempted to shake him had the man not suddenly slipped and fallen headlong across a rock pool. She found herself running to the rocks at last whether Trevor wanted to or not. Indeed, all Trevor did was stay sitting on his mat with his hands over his ears and his eyes shut tight. 'She's seeing ghosts,' he muttered. 'She's pretending there's ghosts again but I'm not frightened. Little boys don't see ghosts.'

39

'Are you all right?' said Helena to the man. One of his feet was all caught up with seaweed so she freed it for him.

'Thank you, my dear,' he said and raised himself stiffly into a sitting position. Then he produced a yellow handkerchief and started mopping his brow. 'Hazardous, looking for props,' he remarked.

'Props?' said Helena, pricking up her ears at once. After all, 'props' was a theatrical term. Was this lucky person in a play?

'We need lots of shells,' he said, 'like this one.' And he held out a big, corkscrewish shell. There was a dent left in the bottom of the pool where he had found it.

'Shall I help you look for them?' said Helena.

'Thank you,' said the man. 'That would be most kind.'

He had a very old-fashioned air which Helena was enjoying. It made her feel that she was acting out a scene with him. While they were searching for shells, she was aware that he kept looking at her. But unlike her experiences with Monica Blaze, it didn't unnerve her. She kept thinking he was about to say something but when she looked at him, his head was down again and he was unearthing a shell. His hair was grey and short and all going backwards. He had it slicked back with something which probably made it look darker than it was.

It wasn't long before they had a pyramid of shells on the rock. The man started stuffing them into his pockets. Helena lay down flat and gazed into a pool.

'Are you . . . er . . . are you in a play?' she asked, chasing a shrimp with her finger.

The man said nothing.

'Are you in a play?' said Helena in a louder voice, thinking he might be a bit deaf.

'Oh, I'm terribly sorry!' said the man, startled. 'I thought you were asking the shrimp. Yes, I'm in a play. The shrimp probably isn't. The question is—would you like to be?'

Helena sat up at once and stared at him. Did he mean it or was he just teasing her?

'We need another player,' he said. 'To play . . . well, a slightly odd part. We haven't found anyone else who could do it. All the other girls auditioned, but they weren't right.'

This was the most exciting thing Helena had ever heard. She was being asked to play a part that nobody else could do.

'It includes a bit of acrobatics,' Henry continued. 'You can do acrobatics, can't you?'

'Yes,' said Helena in a daze.

'I thought you probably could.'

How? wondered Helena. How did he think I probably could?

'We are the Serpenton and High Hat Amateur Theatrical Company,' continued the man. 'I am in charge of it. My name is Henry Mead.' He bowed very low.

'Mine is Helena Woodvine,' said Helena and stood up. She could hardly believe what was happening.

'I'm very pleased to meet you, Helena Woodvine,' said Henry Mead, shaking her hand vigorously, 'and very pleased to welcome you to our amateur theatricals.'

'When do you rehearse?' asked Helena. 'And where?'

'Oh, every day, every day!' said Henry Mead airily, throwing his hands about in magnificent gestures. 'On the beach; on the High Hat; in the—'

'The High Hat?' said Helena. 'That's the hill, isn't it? Behind the village?'

'Correct!' said Mr Mead in his flamboyant way. 'But we won't be rehearsing there tomorrow. We'll be here. On the beach.'

'Why aren't you rehearsing today?' asked Helena.

Henry Mead looked slightly confused.

'Oh . . . er,' he said. 'We . . . er . . . we couldn't rehearse today. We were a player short, you see. But we're not any more, are we? We've found you!'

'Is it . . . er . . . quite a big role?' asked Helena, hardly daring to breathe.

'Oh yes,' said Henry simply. 'It's the lead.'

Helena felt as if she had been handed a massive bouquet . . . and then the sudden cry of a seagull made her look across the sand and she saw . . . she saw Trevor. Trevor! He was still sitting on his mat like a little Buddha. His eyes were still closed.

'Oh, Trevor!' groaned Helena. 'I'd forgotten all about him. Trevor.'

'What ails you?' said Henry Mead, sounding more Shakespearian by the minute. 'Who is this Trevor?'

'He's sitting over there,' said Helena, pointing to the small boy so motionless on his mat. 'I can't be in your play, Mr Mead,' she said woefully. 'I've got to help look after him.'

There was a pause.

'It's more than helping, so far,' she added. 'It's doing all of it.'

'I wonder,' mused Henry and seemed to be thinking for a moment. While he did this, the whole beach seemed to stop. Helena was convinced that if she looked down into the pool again, the shrimp would have frozen in mid-dart. Even the sand seemed to be holding its breath.

'Maybe Monica Blaze could sort something out,' said Henry eventually.

'What do you mean?'

'She could . . . well, you know . . . ' he looked at her but her expression was still blank. 'You've met her, haven't you?' he said.

'Yes,' she said—and then remembered Monica in the shop

and the strange, hypnotic effect she had had on Trevor. A light was starting to dawn . . .

'Will Monica mind?' she asked.

'She will completely understand,' said Henry. 'It has to be done.'

A note of sadness had crept in.

Helena stared at him—but he merely continued.

'I will speak to her tonight,' he said. 'The rehearsal starts at twelve noon tomorrow, so take Trevor to her cottage before then and she'll . . . er . . . see to it that he can come to the rehearsal too—but not be bored and not remember anything about it afterwards.'

'Where's the cottage?' asked Helena at once.

'Oh, that's a point,' said Henry. 'Maybe it won't be the same one as . . . she was living in before . . . '

Helena said nothing, not understanding.

'I can find out,' he said. 'Meet me outside the shop tomorrow morning at about eleven o'clock.'

'All right,' said Helena.

She was beginning to shake with excitement.

CHAPTER SEVEN

Miss Blaze

'Why are we going to Mrs Fields's shop first?' asked Trevor the next morning. 'We're supposed to sit on the beach till lunch-time and then go there.'

He was such a creature of habit, it was unbelievable.

Helena didn't bother answering. She was feeling tense and nervous. He started to drag his steps as they got nearer to the shop so she took a tighter hold of his hand.

'Helena . . . ' he began in his imperious way, 'don't you . . . '

But she had sighted Henry Mead, so she went forward to speak to him, pulling Trevor so hard, he nearly skimmed the pavement with his heels instead of walking.

Henry was very calm.

'I have spoken to her,' he said. 'She'll help.'

'But does she mind?' insisted Helena, aware that she had said this the day before as well.

'No,' said Henry. 'She understands.' He was repeating himself too.

A pause while Helena tried to breathe normally.

'It's the last cottage before the High Hat,' he said. 'Monica will . . . do what's necessary and then both you and Trevor come to the rehearsal—twelve o'clock on the beach, near the long scoop of rock pools. Oh . . . and don't think it's strange if no one seems to acknowledge Trevor. You'll understand when you're there.' And he strode off.

Helena thought it was a bit much him saying the last part of that in front of Trevor himself but then Trevor threw her by remarking, 'Helena, I really will have to tell

Mummy and Daddy about you. You were talking to yourself again!'

She was not putting up with that nonsense today.

'Oh, just be quiet, Trevor and come this way,' she said and started to take him towards the back of the village and the last cottage where Monica Blaze lived. 'The last cottage' had a very final sound to it—it made her think of phrases like 'the last stand' and 'the last survivor' but then she stopped herself. Monica Blaze gave her the creeps enough without working things up for herself even more.

'Where are we going, where are we going?' protested Trevor. 'We should be at the beach!'

It dawned on Helena that to arrive at Monica Blaze's with him in this state was probably not a good idea. She stopped walking.

'We're doing something different today, Trevor,' she said in the 'kind' voice. 'We're going to see that . . . er . . . nice lady called Monica Blaze.'

'Don't want to!'

She ignored that.

Miss Blaze's cottage looked much the same as the others except that she had a twisted, iron window-box on one of the sills. There was something odd about this object—Helena had never seen one like it before. It was like a long snake that was winding round and round itself. There was nothing planted in it. In fact, now she came to think about it, there were no plants or flowers outside anyone else's cottage either. A floating, drifting grey was the only impression that you got.

She realized she was far more nervous about this encounter with Monica than she was about meeting an entire theatre company.

But then meeting an entire theatre company was good training for what she hoped would be her future. Anything to do with baby-sitting was not part of her vision.

45

'What's that?' asked Trevor, looking at the window-box uneasily.

'A window-box,' said Helena, and knocked quickly at the door before her nerve completely failed her.

It was opened at once.

'Good morning,' said Monica Blaze.

'Good morning,' said Helena.

Silence.

Helena swallowed.

'This is very kind of you . . . ' she began in a panic.

'Not really,' said Monica Blaze. 'It's necessary.' Then she looked at Trevor.

'Come in,' she said. 'Step into the hall.'

Trevor began protesting immediately.

'What are we doing here, Helena?' he demanded. 'Why is this person telling me to—'

'This way,' persisted Monica and her voice changed. It had taken on the hypnotic quality Helena had observed in Mrs Fields's shop. It made her shiver slightly.

Trevor still looked uneasy, but stepped into the hall.

'Look at this picture,' said Monica and indicated a large painting on the wall near the foot of the stairs. It had a very jagged frame. Helena couldn't tell whether it was meant to be like that or whether it was broken. She couldn't get any nearer to see because Monica was standing right in front of it with her hands on Trevor's shoulders.

'Look,' she was saying. 'Can you see?'

'Yes,' said Trevor. 'I can see.'

'But what's it a picture of?' asked Helena impatiently.

Monica suddenly flashed her a glance. She had large, almond-shaped brown eyes which startled Helena because they reminded her so much of someone else's.

But whose?

Her mother's?

No, not really.

Whose?

Helena was terribly nervous but she persisted. 'What's it a picture of?'

'The serpent of course.'

'What serpent?'

Monica didn't reply to that: Trevor did.

'Silly Helena,' he said dreamily. 'The sea serpent, of course.'

From a room to the side of them, a clock ticked. Helena hadn't been aware of it before.

'You see,' said Monica. 'Time passes.'

Her statement was very far from original, but it thumped in Helena's head as if it had real meaning. She was aware of a slight dizziness again. Was she being hypnotized herself?

'Trevor,' said Monica, 'will be quite, quite safe.'

A pause.

'Not only that,' She added. 'He will be happy.'

Helena stared at her.

'He will be totally absorbed,' the enigmatic woman continued. 'And nothing is better than that.'

Just below the picture, there was a wooden chest. Monica bent down and opened it. She drew out something which made Helena gasp with pleasure. It was the most beautiful book she had ever seen: it was large and floppy like a scrapbook and the covers were green with an intriguing wiggly pattern and the edges were gold-coloured. She handed it to Trevor who took it without hesitating and put it under his arm. His eyes lit up but he didn't say anything. Then Monica took out a little rucksack which, on opening, proved to have nothing in it but a stack of coloured pencils. Helena watched helplessly while Monica organized things. She took the blue plastic lunch-box and the beach-mat out of Trevor's grasp and put them in the rucksack. The mat stuck out of it like a flag-pole. Then she gently turned him round and put the rucksack over his shoulders. He submitted to all this entirely calmly.

'Now, Trevor,' said Monica, 'here's a book and some pencils. You know what to do with them, don't you?'

Trevor nodded.

'And you know what the theme is, don't you?'

A slow smile spread over his face.

'Right then,' said Monica to Helena. 'Off you go to the rehearsal. Come back here, with the book, when it's over.'

Never had Helena been shown the door so abruptly.

As they were going to the beach, Helena realized that Trevor was equipped for his day out rather like his parents usually were . . . she wondered if he would have more to show for it afterwards . . .

She had a sudden rush of shock and shyness after all as she saw about fifteen people grouped around the line of rock pools. Some were sitting, some standing—one sprawling. The sprawling one was the younger of the two girls Helena had seen on the beach the other day. The older one was there too, talking to Henry Mead. They were wearing the flowery dresses again.

Meanwhile, Trevor, with a sudden movement that made Helena jump, plonked himself down on the sand, took the rucksack off his back, opened it, took out some pencils, spread his scrap-book out and started to draw. Helena stood for a moment staring at him—then realized that he, unlike her, was sorting himself out for the day. He gave no indication whatsoever that he had seen anyone else on the beach . . .

Helena made herself look at the theatre company—and the group seemed like a shot from a film. Then Henry Mead detached himself from the group and came towards her.

Everything became more real. The people he drew her among were smiling and nodding at her. He got her as far as the rock pools before he spoke.

'We'll start with my daughters,' he said simply.

'I've seen them before!' said Helena. 'On the beach. The other day.'

They both smiled at her.

'This is Imogen,' said Henry, indicating the older one, 'and this is Julia.'

'Hello,' said Julia. 'When we saw you the other day, we wondered if you were the one.'

'The one?' asked Helena.

'She means someone we could ask to be in the play,' said Imogen swiftly. 'We thought you looked as if you could do it.'

'Yes,' said Julia, 'we were sure you could. You'll probably do it better than M—'

At that, Imogen nudged her hard and smiled very brightly at Helena. Julia looked rather sheepish.

Helena then saw someone else she recognized.

'Hello again,' she said to the pieman.

'Hello,' he said. 'I'm sorry about the confusion the other day. I'm not really a pieman, you see. This is just my costume. I'm a pieman in the play.'

'And he couldn't tell you that before,' put in Julia, 'because he didn't know you were going to be in the play too!'

But why, thought Helena. What was wrong with him telling me, whether I was going to be in it too or not?

Maybe she was imagining it but there seemed to be a lull in proceedings—enough time for a seagull to land on the rocks so close to her that she jumped.

Imogen broke into this by calling over to someone:

'Meggy, stop skulking about over there! Come and meet Helena!'

49

Another girl, about Helena's age, came rather hesitantly towards them. She too was in a flowery dress of uncertain length and fabric.

Where do they get them? thought Helena. The shop hasn't got it quite right.

'This is Meggy Johnson,' said Imogen firmly.

Meggy was much shyer than either Imogen or Julia. But Helena did notice that she was the only one in the whole company who cast any sort of glance in Trevor's direction. She was immediately given a dig in the ribs by Imogen and made to look away again.

'It is nice to be back, isn't it?' said somebody suddenly—and, to Helena's surprise, a lot of the others glared really hard at him. He went crimson. 'I'm sorry, I didn't think,' he mumbled. There was a pause. Then most of them started talking very bright and fast like a lot of coloured beads being shaken about. Helena was completely bewildered by this time. It must have been noticed because the next thing she knew was somebody taking her by the shoulders and calling on everyone else to be quiet. It was Henry Mead.

'This is our new player,' he said. 'Her name is Helena Woodvine and she will be playing the part of Stoney Vale.'

Then they all clapped and cheered.

This was very gratifying to Helena. This might all happen professionally one day, she thought.

'Sit down, everyone,' said Henry. 'Time we got started. Miss Smith, can you hand out the scripts please?'

Miss Smith was a smallish, middle-aged woman who had been standing silently while most of the others were behaving like coloured beads. For some reason, she seemed to be in charge of the scripts. She had them in a bag like a music case.

'Oh yes, here you are,' she said dully and handed them out.

Helena looked at hers eagerly. Her heart was beating very fast.

The read-through began. 'Stoney Vale' didn't appear in the opening scenes and Helena was amazed at how quickly and confidently the others got through their lines—as if they had done them countless times before. She wondered just how long they had been waiting for a 'Stoney Vale' to turn up. When it came to the parts that she was in, they slowed down a bit to give her a chance but she still felt odd and out on a limb. Another thing—the main thing really—was that she liked the play at once. More than liked it. She thought it was wonderful. It was set in Serpenton itself at a time which Helena couldn't quite define—but it didn't seem to matter.

For the second time that morning, Helena heard mention of a 'sea serpent'—which explained what Monica was on about earlier. It sent a shiver down her spine. The sea serpent, it seemed, was a myth of the village that inspired the play. The playwright (or someone further back in the past) had decided that that was why the place was called Serpenton.

In the play, everyone believed in the sea serpent—but no one ever seemed to see him. They treated him as a sort of god: they threw flowers into the sea for him.

Stoney Vale, the character Helena was playing, was extraordinary. 'Stoney' was not her real name—but it was what everyone called her ever since someone had said that talking to her was like talking to a stone wall. This was because she quite often didn't respond traditionally. She was dreamy and slightly wild and people didn't really understand her. She had three friends but even they didn't know how to deal with her sometimes. The friends were played by Imogen and Julia Mead and Meggy Johnson.

One day, a travelling fair came to Serpenton and the young people were all captivated by the tumblers. Afterwards, there was a scene where they all tried to do gymnastics themselves but Stoney was the only one who could. So, in spite of themselves, a note of admiration started to creep into the way they treated her. Someone said she was as supple as the sea serpent—even though he had never been sighted.

Then Stoney started disappearing for hours on end. On returning, she kept saying she was 'with the serpent, with the serpent'. The serpent—that no one else had ever seen! And she brought things back—rare shells and unusual stones which made you gasp to look at. Stoney Vale changed, in the people's eyes, from being an enigmatic child to an exciting celebrity.

At the end of the play, she gave her precious shells and stones away—one to each person as if to say 'goodbye'. She was trembling with a curious excitement. She went off to the beach and was never seen or heard of again. The last line of the script was someone saying 'If it's true that she was seeing the serpent, she's with him forever now.'

A drowned body was never found.

At the end of the read-through, Helena was in tears. So were a lot of the others which was remarkable because it wasn't new to them like it was to her. There was a curious glamour about the part of 'Stoney Vale' even though she was odd. It was the most appealing role Helena had ever been cast in. She wondered, actually, if there was going to be any resentment from the other three girls who had auditioned, but hadn't got the part. If there was, then they weren't showing it yet.

The only person who seemed completely unmoved by the reading was Miss Smith who had given out the scripts at the beginning. 'That was nice,' she said blandly. For some reason, Helena wanted to shake her hard.

They had a short break and then started to walk through the scenes. At least, it was 'walking through' for Helena.

Everyone else seemed to know exactly what they were doing already. 'Running through' was more what they were doing.

One thing that puzzled Helena was that the man who played a young lover wasn't that young. His 'girlfriend' was in her late twenties but he was at least forty-five. He wore very round glasses with very thick lenses. Didn't they have any younger men in Serpenton? thought Helena. She was still feeling as if she herself had achieved hardly anything when Henry said, 'All right, that'll be it for the day.'

They had been rehearsing for about three hours.

Everyone started to pack up their things and get ready to go.

'Goodbye, Helena,' said Imogen pleasantly.

'I'm really glad you've joined the company,' said Julia and a lot of the others said similar things. Meggy Johnson only smiled shyly but Helena knew she meant the same. Miss Smith said nothing and did nothing.

'I just want to ask something,' said Helena to Imogen. 'Does anyone believe in the serpent now?'

'Of course not!' said Imogen and laughed.

It was only then that Helena realized she was completely exhausted.

Bit by bit, they all disappeared—except Henry Mead.

'Very good for a first day,' he said.

Helena's head suddenly started to swim. She sat down unsteadily on the rocks.

'Yes,' said Henry quietly. 'It will make you feel like that.' He put his hand on her shoulder. 'Now,' he said. 'Time you saw to Trevor . . . '

And he strode off as nonchalantly as he had earlier when they were outside Mrs Fields's shop.

Helena was struck with horror as she realized that she had practically forgotten Trevor all through the rehearsal . . . But she needn't have worried. She looked over at him and saw he was lying stretched right out, drawing in his scrap-book—as Monica had predicted, completely absorbed. He hadn't even bothered to spread out the mat he was usually so concerned about and one of his feet was sticking up in the air. Helena went to him and shook the foot gently.

Immediately he sat up and turned to face her. Helena gasped in astonishment, all her daze from the rehearsal dispelling. His eyes, though fixed, were shining—and if ever she was to see an intensely joyful face, she was looking at it now.

She didn't get a chance to look in the book; he snapped it shut.

A little later, when Monica Blaze opened the door to them, she looked at Helena quizzically—but then, that was nothing new.

'How was the . . . rehearsal?' she asked—and it seemed she had some trouble saying 'rehearsal'.

'Oh . . . all right,' said Helena.

She felt the need to be cautious: today had gone quite well but tomorrow might not. 'Stoney Vale' was not to be taken on lightly.

Monica stared at her fixedly for a few moments.

Whose eyes are like hers? wondered Helena again—but then their gaze was transferred to Trevor. He smiled and handed Monica the scrap-book. She opened it and smiled as well.

'He likes the sea serpent then,' she said.

So, at the same time as Helena was being Stoney Vale obsessed by the serpent, Trevor was drawing pictures about the same myth. She wanted to tell Monica this.

'The play's about the sea serpent,' she began. 'And—'
Monica stopped her.

'Do you really think,' she said icily, 'that I do not know what the play's about? Me—of all people?'

Helena was shocked, not knowing what to say.

'Same time tomorrow, I presume,' said Monica and shut the door.

Had it been anyone else, Helena would have called that rude—but Monica seemed rather upset.

Trevor held on to Helena's hand as they walked home. The shine and joy had gone from his face now, which made Helena feel rather sad, but he still seemed quite contented.

'Did . . . did you enjoy your day?' she asked him.

'Well, you should know,' said Trevor peacefully. 'You were there.'

'But . . . er . . . I wasn't playing with you,' said Helena. 'You were drawing pictures on your own.'

'Don't be silly,' said Trevor and started to hum a cheerful little tune.

So he remembers nothing at all, thought Helena. Suddenly she was filled with panic. What was she doing to him? Was she allowing him to be hypnotized by a strange woman who seemed to have several chips on her shoulder as well?

But then she remembered how startlingly joyful his face had been—and then, like a strain of weird music in her brain, she remembered how being Stoney Vale had made her feel and she did not want to stop doing it. It'll be all right, it'll be all right, she thought. Henry said so. I believe him.

'What did you do today, Trevor darling?' asked Christine.

'Sssssh, Mummy,' said Trevor, not taking his eyes away from the television screen. 'The monster's just asking the girl to marry him.'

'Don't tell Mummy to be quiet, darling,' said Christine

with just a hint of something explosive in her voice, 'or you mightn't get any chicken for dinner.'

'We went to the beach,' said Trevor at once.

'That's nice, dear,' said Christine and put a bowl of chicken and rice on his knees. She put a spoon in his hand. Trevor ate everything with a spoon—even things with lumps. Everything was cut up very small for him, as if he were still a baby.

'Now, Helena,' said Christine in a very wheedling sort of voice, 'I know we said we wouldn't do this again but would you mind awfully staying in with Trevor this evening? You see, we've been asked round for drinks with our new friends. Delightful couple, aren't they, Robin?'

'Yes,' said Robin with his mouth full.

'And really, it might look a bit rude to refuse and we thought . . . '

'Oh that's all right!' said Helena brightly and Christine stared at her in amazement. She had never agreed so readily before.

But Helena didn't want to go out this evening. She wanted to stay at home and study the part of Stoney Vale.

CHAPTER EIGHT

In The Village Hall

The next morning, on the way to Monica's, Helena was surprised to observe that Trevor wasn't kicking up any sort of fuss about not going in the direction of the beach. She decided to experiment.

'We're not going to the beach today, Trevor,' she said.

His grip on her hand didn't tighten or loosen.

'Really?' he said peacefully and strolled along.

'Or Monica Blaze's house either,' she lied.

'Aren't we?'

'No.'

Pause.

'What are we doing then?' he asked with just a slight crack in his voice.

Helena looked at him. Was this the cue for him to lapse into his usual imperiousness or not?

She thought of the thing he was most likely to object to.

'We're going to climb the High Hat,' she announced dramatically, pointing ahead of them to the hill that rose up at the end of the road.

There was a silence.

Trevor stopped and let go of her hand.

This is when he'll revert to normal, she thought.

She stared at him.

He chewed his lip.

'Do we have to?' he asked in a wavering voice very far from imperious.

Helena was so shocked by this abnormal reaction, she didn't say anything but grabbed his hand again and made him walk.

Monica was actually waiting for them outside her house.

'Oh . . . are we late?' asked Helena in alarm.

'No,' said Monica—and Helena realized she was leaning her head against the wall in the sun. She was sitting on a wooden chair with her grey hair brushing against the empty, snaky window-box. This image of an 'older' woman in the sun made her think, slightly longingly, of her mother.

But she pushed that aside immediately.

Tender thoughts of her mother! How ridiculous. She didn't like her.

Monica rose to her feet and looked steadily at Trevor. Helena felt his hand start to slip out of hers. He took a step forward.

'Would you like to hear more about the sea serpent?' asked Monica—and her voice was so compelling that Helena found herself answering, 'Yes please.'

'No, no, not you!' snapped Monica, her tone changing immediately.

Helena blinked.

Monica had opened the house and the hallway was like a throat swallowing Trevor. Helena followed quickly—before the front door could close like a mouth with her on the other side of it. Again, Trevor was put into a kind of daze and handed the scrap-book and pencils. Again, Helena was told rather abruptly to leave for the rehearsal. When they came out, Henry Mead was waiting outside. He looked rather agitated.

'You needn't have met me!' said Helena in concern. 'You'll have to walk all the way back down to the beach now.'

'Well, no,' said Henry rather oddly. 'We're not rehearsing there today. Didn't I tell you?'

'Where are we going then?'

'To . . . to the village hall,' he said and she wondered what it was that made him gnaw at his lip.

'The village hall?' said Helena, puzzled. 'I don't remember seeing a village hall anywhere.'

'Er . . . no, you wouldn't have,' said Henry carefully. 'Not unless you knew.'

'Knew what?'

'Its location. It was built on top of a hill. I mean, it is built on top of a hill.'

'How strange,' said Helena.

'Yes it is, isn't it?' said Henry. 'It was built by a rich Victorian eccentric. As far as I know, it wasn't done for any reason other than he just fancied putting it there.'

The road past Monica's house bent round slightly to the right and a smallish hill rose abruptly in front of them. The day was very warm and pleasant and the grass on the slopes was very green and clovery. Did this by any chance include four-leafed ones? thought Helena.

'This is High Hat Hill,' said Henry and still he was being odd about something. Maybe he just couldn't be bothered to climb it, thought Helena—and indeed, he made very slow work of it. She could have looked for several four-leafed clovers in the time and she kept wanting to run circles round him and say 'Come on, Henry,'—but she couldn't be rude to the director of the theatre company. Trevor sat down a few times thinking it was time to start drawing in his scrap-book—but before he could get his pencils out, Henry moved on again. When they were very nearly at the top, Henry stumbled slightly. It was only a very small catch of the foot, not enough to make him fall—but still he sat down heavily and put his head in his hands. Trevor sat down again too. He opened his scrap-book.

'Did you hurt your foot, Henry?' asked Helena.

'No,' said Henry. 'It's not my foot that hurts.'

He didn't explain any further. A couple of minutes later, he got up again. Without being asked, so did Trevor.

The top of the hill was quite thickly wooded. It was a bit of a shock to come upon the village hall in the middle of it. It hadn't been visible from the bottom of the hill. Waiting among the trees were the players. Henry and Helena were the last to arrive. Once again, Helena saw the scene as a frozen image—like a snapshot from the past. They were grouped around the trees at different head-levels—some sitting, some standing. No one had actually attempted to climb one as Helena might have done. Stoney Vale would have done, too, of course . . . It was odd really. You would have thought that with a group of over ten people, some of them would have been seen from below—especially the girls in their flowery dresses—but Helena hadn't seen them.

'They must have appeared from nowhere,' she said lightly to Henry, expecting him to laugh and say 'don't be silly', but he didn't. He just looked at her.

She felt panic begin to rise again.

'It's because they're keeping so still, isn't it?' she said.

In a group that was moving about, you would expect to see a flash of bright fabric sticking through a gap in the trees, or the pieman's tray or someone's legs. But there had been nothing.

Trevor wasn't thinking about it though. This time when he sat down, there was time to get his pencils out.

There seemed to be a general state of agitation among the players. Meggy Johnson kept giving fearful glances at the village hall.

'Now come on, everyone,' said Henry, trying to be brisk and efficient—but you could tell he was as agitated as anyone else. 'Time we all . . . er . . . went in and started rehearsing.'

A gasp went up from the company.

'You must understand how we feel, Dad,' said Imogen's cool voice.

'Yes, yes, I understand,' said Henry. But Helena didn't. What were they going on about?

'Here goes,' said Imogen and she walked up to the door and flung it open. Everyone shifted back a pace or two. But nothing extraordinary happened! The door was creaking in a perfectly ordinary way—it opened into a cool room with a raised platform at one end and chairs arranged in neat rows in front of it. There was a piano to one side of the platform. An old-fashioned-looking poster was stuck on one of the walls.

Everyone just stood and looked.

Oh this is ridiculous, thought Helena finally and stepped into the hall herself. She took a look at the poster and saw it was a Second World War one she had heard her father talk about and also seen in the War Museum in London. The slogan was 'Careless talk costs lives'. Why that one, she thought. Why do they want that on the wall?

Imogen had followed her in.

'It's all right!' she said to the others, holding her arms out as if she were somehow 'feeling' the place. 'Nothing's happened to me!'

One by one, they all trooped in. Trevor brought up the rear—and at last was able to settle. He went right into a corner and started to draw. But the rehearsal was running for about half an hour before Helena felt that everyone else was properly settled. And even then, she wasn't sure about Meggy. But she was too busy worrying about Stoney Vale to ask any questions about anything else.

Things didn't go so well for her today. They were rehearsing a scene where Stoney walked on her hands for at least a minute, and it really did seem that most of them expected her to do it immediately. They cleared a space for her—and then just stood and waited. Helena went crimson. Right! she thought, here goes—and she threw herself into a handstand, staggered about upside-down for a couple of seconds and then fell sideways.

'Er . . . I haven't done gymnastics for a while,' she said from a sitting position.

'Never mind,' said Henry. 'Try again.'

The second time she managed to walk two or three paces on her hands but backwards.

'I don't know why, but my hands keep wanting to go this way,' she said.

'The trouble is,' said Imogen, 'that Stoney Vale went forwards. It says so in the script.'

Helena could feel her temper beginning to rise.

'Why don't you show me how it's done then?' she said rather shortly.

'Oh, I can't do gymnastics,' said Imogen. 'Nobody here can except you. That's why you got the part.'

This silenced Helena. After all, she had to remember that Imogen, Julia, and Meggy had all gone for the part and not got it. It didn't occur to her to wonder how they had all been so sure she could do gymnastics. Nobody had asked her to do an audition or anything. She tried again. This time, she went backwards for three steps and then forced herself forward for one. Then she fell right over into a 'crab'. Luckily, she managed to get upright again without looking too awkward.

She was just about to throw herself into it again when Henry said, 'That'll do for now. We'll go on to something else.' Then she had to sit to one side while they rehearsed a scene that she wasn't in.

It seemed to Helena that no one else was having any trouble with anything at all. They all glided through their lines and seemed to know exactly where to move without being told. She hoped it was because they had been rehearsing a lot and not because they were all naturally brilliant.

At one point, Meggy came and sat next to her and whispered, 'Are you all right?' Instantly, the tears were in

Helena's eyes like little wet traitors. She nodded her head savagely and hoped that Meggy would either go away or not notice—or preferably both. Meggy went away.

The next thing that occurred to Helena was when on earth was someone going to suggest they stopped for lunch? She was so hungry that if they had asked her to do another handstand, she would have crumpled to the floor. But the rehearsal was going on and on and no one else was showing any signs of hunger at all. Most of them had terribly rapt expressions on their faces as if anything as vulgar as sandwiches could not possibly enter the beautiful mind of an actor. For a moment, Helena didn't know what she wanted more; food, or to be involved in the rehearsal again and be at one with the others. The answer came to her very swiftly; she wanted food.

And Trevor ought to be administered to as well.

But when she got over to his corner, she found that he had sorted this out for himself. His blue plastic lunch-box was open and he was taking the last but one bite of his last sandwich. Helena was treated to a tantalizing flash of yellow cheese—and then the last bite was gone as well. Very composedly, Trevor shut up the blue plastic box and went, with a deep sigh of satisfaction, back to his drawing. Helena was left on her own with her lunch.

Unfortunately, she was not someone who found it easy to eat in public—not unless everyone else was eating as well. She tried to think of the easiest item in her sandwich box. The sandwiches themselves were out of the question; they were too full of chunks of tomato or uneven lumps of cheese. They might fall out when she was taking a bite and be really embarrassing. The chocolate wouldn't do either—it might have melted. In the end, she decided the banana would be the safest thing—and she reached for it surreptitiously in her rucksack.

She became so absorbed in eating it that she didn't notice the rehearsal had finally stopped. She didn't notice that everyone was staring at her very oddly—or rather, they were not so much staring at her as at the banana. When she did become aware, she stopped eating it and went bright red.

'I . . . I'm sorry,' she mumbled. 'I was hungry.'

They all pulled themselves together again.

'Oh, we didn't mean to stare,' said Imogen.

'It's just that we haven't seen a b—' began Julia but Imogen gave her such a nudge that she clapped a hand over her mouth as if she had said something stupid—and never finished the sentence.

'You're quite right, Helena,' said Henry. 'It is time we had a break.' He promptly sat down exactly where he was on the floor. Some of the others did the same. Imogen wandered outside.

It was a very false kind of break. They all just sat there politely and didn't say anything. The scratch and swish of Trevor's pencils suddenly sounded very loud. Helena got the feeling that if they hadn't caught her eating the banana they would never have stopped at all. She felt worse and worse. And still nobody was eating. They all carried those lunch-box things around with them but nobody opened one and took out any provisions. After about ten minutes, Henry said, 'Have you had enough lunch, Helena?'

'Yes thank you,' she lied—and they all got up to begin the rehearsal again. In her embarrassed confusion, Helena had left the banana skin lying on the floor without meaning to—and, of course, one of the cast had to slip on it and fall flat on his back. Julia seemed to find this rather amusing but for Helena it was the last straw. All she wanted now was a theatrical trapdoor to open just under her feet—but the Serpenton and High Hat village hall didn't have one.

At about three o'clock, Henry suddenly said, 'Oh, Helena, you'd better go! Time to take Trevor back to Monica's.'

Helena looked confused.

'Isn't the rehearsal ending for the rest of you then?'

'I think the rest of us will stay here a little longer,' said Henry and everyone looked very enthusiastic at the idea.

'Goodbye then,' said Helena in a small voice. 'Er . . . see you tomorrow.'

'See you tomorrow,' they all said and plunged straight back into the rehearsal again.

Helena made her way very dangerously back down the hill because she was blinded by tears. She kept Trevor in front of her. At the bottom, she got her handkerchief out and scrubbed fiercely at her eyes. He waited politely, still in a kind of trance. Then she opened her sandwich box and stuffed half a sandwich in her mouth in one go. Before they were half-way to Monica's, she had eaten all the others as well—and the bar of chocolate.

That night, still in a state of depression, she sat in her bedroom at the cottage, watching the black and white portable television that was there.

The screen flickered unstably at her but she was too low-spirited to care about adjusting it. She left it on while she ran a bath only because she couldn't be bothered to turn it off. But when she re-emerged from the bathroom, she was suddenly transfixed by what had come on in the meantime.

It was a forties' film.

She had been in the bath about twenty minutes so the basic setting was established. The scene she came in on was a group of people in a café. Helena gasped when she saw it. She was only wearing a towel and her hair was dripping down her back but she stayed like that, drawn to the screen.

The players in the café scene looked a very similar group

to the members of the theatre company. There were some young girls in flowery dresses with buttons down the front.

Helena sat down on the floor. The towel slipped off her and her wet hair was cold on her back but she barely noticed.

She suddenly leaned forward and turned the television off.

'What a coincidence,' she said rather shakily.

CHAPTER NINE

Walking On Your Hands

The next morning, Helena got up early and went down to the beach to practise hand-walking. She was surprised to see footsteps in the sand as if someone had got there even earlier. They went up to the rock pools and then back again—and they were accompanied by another sort of mark—a small, round hole in the firm sand which went with them all the way.

Helena wasted no time but tipped herself into a handstand immediately. The sand felt cool and gritty under her palms. She walked forward for two steps, put her right hand accidentally on a sharp piece of shell and shouted with pain. She startled two seagulls who screamed themselves into the air and, of course, she came down abruptly from the handstand. She sucked at the palm of her hand which was bleeding.

'Put this on it and start again,' said a voice behind her. Helena jumped violently and jerked her head round. Miss Monica Blaze was standing there with her walking cane in one hand and holding out a piece of sticking plaster in the other.

'I always carry a first aid kit with me,' she explained.

'Thank you,' said Helena and took the plaster.

'Wash the cut first,' ordered Miss Blaze. 'The salt water will be good for it.'

Helena went up to the rocks, making more footsteps to go with the ones already there. She now realized the other ones must belong to Miss Blaze—and the small, round ones were made by the end of her walking cane. Helena dipped her hand in one of the rock pools, dried it on her handkerchief and covered the cut with the plaster. She could feel Miss Blaze's eyes on her all the time. Then she walked back.

'Try some more hand-walking,' said Monica Blaze.

Feeling incredibly stupid, Helena went obediently into another handstand.

'Arch more,' said Miss Blaze. 'Your back has to arch and your legs curve over. No, no, don't bend your knees.'

Helena tried to do as she said but fell over sideways. She tried again and did better this time. She actually walked on her hands for seven steps.

'There you are,' said Miss Blaze triumphantly. 'You've just got to arch!'

Then, suddenly and inexplicably, her face clouded over.

'I used to walk on my hands,' she said. 'But I'm too old now.' She looked at Helena with the strange half-hostility she had shown before. 'Do you like being in the play?' she asked rather aggressively.

'I enjoyed the read-through,' said Helena. 'But yesterday's rehearsal went all wrong.'

'How did it go wrong?' asked Miss Blaze and she sounded almost eager as if this could make her feel better. Helena was rather offended.

'Oh, I don't know,' she muttered. 'It was mainly the hand-walking, I suppose.'

And then Miss Blaze seemed to relent again.

'Stoney Vale is a very difficult part,' she said.

'Do you know it then?' asked Helena in surprise.

'Of course!' cried Monica Blaze but she didn't explain how she knew it. 'I want my breakfast,' she said. 'I'll see you later when you bring Trevor,' she added and walked off.

If she were younger, thought Helena, I would say she was acting as if she were jealous!

She then spent another half hour walking on her hands and got the score up to eleven steps—but that was only once. Then she went home to get Trevor.

The rehearsal was in the village hall again today—and when it came to the hand-walking scene, Helena walked for six steps and all in the right direction. She was disappointed because it wasn't as many as she had managed that morning but everyone else clapped and said 'Well done'. Maybe they were feeling they had been a bit hard on her yesterday.

'You've been practising, haven't you?' said Henry, and he sounded pleased.

'Yes,' said Helena—but she said nothing about the strange episode with Monica Blaze. Something stopped her from mentioning it though she didn't know what.

She went home that evening feeling much happier. Time, therefore, for a bit of dreaming. She didn't say a word all through supper because she was too busy imagining that someone 'important' would come and see the play and say it should go to the West End. So Helena would be Stoney Vale in a London theatre . . . which would become as prized a part as Saint Joan or something (another extraordinary character) . . . and instead of the modest platform in the village hall, there would be a big, high stage and the heavy, red swirl of a curtain and lots of greasepaint starting to run under the lights . . .

CHAPTER TEN

Miss Smith's Handkerchief

Next day, the rehearsal was on the beach which Helena much preferred to the village hall. She enjoyed going up the hill but there was definitely something odd about the hall itself—which, she thought, was the reason why they couldn't face rehearsing there every day. On the beach, she felt much more relaxed and she thought that most of the others did as well—especially Meggy Johnson.

Trevor today didn't just stick to his coloured pencils; Helena could see out the corner of her eye that he was flourishing twists of dried seaweed as well. A little pot of clear, brown glue had appeared in the rucksack along with the pencils. Meggy, Helena noticed, still looked at him now and then with a doting expression in her eyes. Maybe she was one of those people who fantasize about having children very early . . . Everyone else still continued to ignore him totally. Helena wondered if they might actually be rather selfish or ruthless—but quickly dismissed that idea. She could understand the driving force of a theatrical 'cause'.

On this particular day, Helena found herself getting more and more annoyed with Miss Smith. For one thing, she never seemed to do anything but stand about and say, 'That's nice,' in a voice as dull as a ditch. Helena just couldn't understand why she was part of the theatre company. 'I've lost my handkerchief,' she was moaning today. 'I always have my handkerchief about me but today I haven't got it.'

'Perhaps you've dropped it somewhere,' suggested the man who played the pieman (his real name was Solomon)—and then Henry commanded that the rehearsal be stopped while they combed their pitch of beach for it. Helena could hardly believe it! Stop a rehearsal for a mere handkerchief! When they failed to find it, Miss Smith seemed to be in such a state of distress that Helena burst out with, 'Why don't you go to the shop and buy another one?'

'Go . . . go to the shop?' faltered Miss Smith.

'Yes,' said Helena. 'Mrs Fields's shop.'

'Mrs Fields!' said Miss Smith. 'It does sound odd to hear that slip of a thing being called that. I still think of her as Mary Jackson.'

'Well, she's only been married about a week!' said Julia. 'You'll soon get used to her new n—' She stopped talking and looked rather odd.

'Yes, Julia,' said Imogen drily. 'You never think before you open your mouth, do you?'

Helena was completely bewildered.

'I think you're getting muddled up with someone else,' she said. 'Mrs Fields isn't a young slip of a thing who's only just got married! She must be about seventy!'

'Seventy!' gasped Miss Smith. She gave a low moan and sat down on a rock. 'Yes,' she said dismally. 'I suppose she would be seventy.'

'The other thing is,' said Imogen—and she sounded rather subdued for her—'is that her husband was probably . . . well, you know, killed.' And then, with a hasty look at Helena, she changed that to 'I mean, he probably died.'

Helena didn't want to think about this. Disturbing thoughts were beginning to haunt her about these people— and she was doing her utmost to suppress them. She felt an almost ridiculous desperation about playing Stoney Vale. It had to happen regardless of anything else.

'Well anyway,' she said, trying to bring things back to normal, 'why don't you go and buy a handkerchief from Mrs Fields? I'm sure she'll have some.'

'Oh, I couldn't! I couldn't!' wailed Miss Smith. 'Not to see a woman who's seventy when I remember Mary Jackson!'

'I'll tell you what, Helena,' cut in Henry, 'you're not in the next scene, are you? Maybe you wouldn't mind going to get Miss Smith a handkerchief?'

'I really can't manage without one, you see,' whined Miss Smith. Helena felt the usual urge to shake her hard.

'What about Trevor?' she asked.

'Oh, I'll keep an eye on him,' said Meggy at once and then went bright red because everyone stared.

'Can you give me the money then?' Helena asked Miss Smith.

'Oh, yes, I suppose so,' said Miss Smith and, very slowly, she brought out a small, leather purse from her pocket. She shook out three large brown coins and was about to hand them to Helena when Imogen rushed in and snatched them from her.

'Oh, Miss Smith!' cried Imogen. 'This won't do at all! I mean . . .' and she cast a meaningful look at her father.

'Er . . . no, no, of course not,' said Henry. 'That money will be no good . . . er, I mean the theatre company will pay for it, Miss Smith.'

Miss Smith looked relieved.

'How kind,' she said. 'They were my three last pen—'

'Helena's waiting to go, Dad,' said Imogen rather loudly.

'Oh yes, of course,' said Henry and he took Helena to one side. 'This is a bit awkward,' he said apologetically. 'But we haven't really got any money. Could you say to . . . er . . . Mrs Fields that Henry Mead from the theatre company would like a handkerchief for Miss Smith and I'm sure she'd understand.'

'Give you one without paying for it, you mean?' said Helena.

72

Henry flushed.

'Er . . . yes,' he said. 'I suppose I do mean that.'

'All right then,' said Helena ungraciously and made as if to go.

'One more thing, Helena,' said Henry, laying his hand on her shoulder.

The tone of his voice arrested her. Was he going to be terribly critical about her performance that morning? He cleared his throat. Helena's heart sank lower.

'I . . . er . . . I know we sometimes take against people for no particular reason,' he said. 'It happens to us all. But do you think you could try and be a bit more . . . tolerant towards Miss Smith, Helena? After all, we couldn't do without her—and she's had to do a lot of miserable hanging around, you know.'

Helena didn't know what he meant by that. Miss Smith didn't have a part in the play and if she didn't like 'hanging around', then why was she always there? She had had no idea that her dislike of her was so obvious.

'I'm sorry,' she muttered.

'Hello, Helena!' said Mrs Fields. 'I haven't seen you for a few days.'

'I've been rehearsing,' said Helena. 'I'm in a play. Did you know?'

'Oh yes,' said Mrs Fields, 'and I'm looking forward to it.'

Something occurred to Helena that hadn't before.

'Who is there to come and see it?' she asked in alarm. 'I never seem to see anyone else in Serpenton.'

'Just because *you* never see them,' said Mrs Fields quietly, 'it doesn't mean that they're not there.'

Helena shivered. It wasn't an unpleasant sort of shiver but suddenly she wanted to sit down. She looked round rather wildly for a chair. There wasn't one.

'The floor's quite clean,' said Mrs Fields.

Helena sank down on it at once.

'Now, what can I do for you?' said Mrs Fields. She sounded like her usual comfortable self again. Helena was relieved.

'It's something for someone from the theatre company,' she said from the floor. 'Do you know Miss Smith?'

'Yes,' said Mrs Fields.

'Do you like her? Oh, that's not relevant! It just came out. I mean, she needs a handkerchief and Henry Mead said do you think you could let . . . '

'Yes of course,' said Mrs Fields and she brought out several from under the counter.

After Helena had chosen one and was about to leave, Mrs Fields said, 'I know what you mean about Miss Smith—but she's been kept waiting so long, you know. You have to bear with her.'

'So long for what?' said Helena. 'If you mean waiting for someone to turn up to play my part, then she's not the only one, is she? The others have been waiting too and they don't act like she does.'

'But it's her baby, isn't it?' said Mrs Fields.

'What do you mean?' said Helena who was not familiar with that expression unless you meant a real baby.

'You'll see,' said Mrs Fields.

When she got back to the beach with the handkerchief, Helena tried to be nicer to Miss Smith. 'Here you are!' she said cheerfully, handing the handkerchief to her. 'I chose the brightest one!' The handkerchief was scarlet.

'Oh dear, yes, you did, didn't you?' said Miss Smith. 'Well, it was very nice of you, Helen, but I'm afraid I—'

'Helena,' said Helena, her resolution to be nicer to Miss Smith beginning to slip already.

'I beg your pardon?'

'I think you know perfectly well that my name isn't Helen. It's Helena—with an "a" on the end.'

'Well, I'm very sorry, Helena,' said Miss Smith stiffly—and the letter 'a' fell out of her mouth like a bomb, 'but I'm afraid I couldn't think of using a bright red handkerchief. It's much too garish for me.'

Helena nearly exploded. She was just about to snatch the offending square of scarlet from Miss Smith's fingers when someone put his hand on her shoulder. She spun round, saw it was Henry, was savaged instantly with guilt and went straight off to the shop to get another one.

This time, she got a beige one.

'Thank you,' said Miss Smith and blew her nose on it at once.

That afternoon, they dealt with one of the scenes where Stoney Vale was teased by the other three girls, before they discovered she could do acrobatics.

Before they started, Imogen informed them that she was just in the right mood for playing this scene because Julia had been annoying her all day and she could pass on the feeling to Stoney Vale. Julia looked sulky and Helena felt terrified. Consequently, it really did go rather well. The rest of the company watched them, spellbound, and when the scene ended, there was first an awed silence—and then they all clapped.

'We're getting on,' said Henry excitedly. 'That's the best I've ever seen it played!'

But then Meggy spoilt it all. She seemed to lose heart. In the next scene with the four of them, her lines came out lamer and lamer. To compensate for this, Imogen got harsher and harsher—and Julia always followed Imogen's lead. Helena, as Stoney Vale, was very nearly reduced to a gibbering wreck.

'Come, come now!' said Henry, clapping his hands and stopping them. 'Whatever's happened now? It was so good in the last scene. What have you done to it?'

'It's Meggy,' said Imogen at once. 'She's not putting any heart into her lines. I have to be extra menacing to make up for it.'

'Well, don't be,' said her father. 'You're going right over the top. And Meggy, start doing it properly again please. We have to get the balance right or these scenes won't work at all.'

To everyone's amazement, Meggy burst into tears.

'I can't, I can't!' she sobbed. 'I can't be nasty to Helena.'

'But you're not being nasty to Helena,' said Henry impatiently. 'You're being nasty to Stoney Vale.'

'But it's the same thing!' Meggy wailed. 'Helena makes it so real! I keep on thinking she really is upset! It wasn't like that when M—'

'The other person did it,' Imogen finished for her.

'Who was that?' asked Helena curiously.

'Oh . . . a girl called Veronica,' said Imogen swiftly. 'But she had to drop out. That's why we got you.'

'You weren't going to say "Veronica" though, were you, Meggy?' said Helena, puzzled. 'I thought the name began with an . . .'

'Meggy got it wrong,' said Imogen.

The company went on to rehearse a scene that none of the four girls was in. They all did different things instead. Imogen sat down to watch the other players and criticize; Julia gathered up a load of seaweed and sat a little way off, popping the purple blisters between her fingers. But then one burst rather loudly and Imogen told her to stop. She didn't—but turned her back on Imogen and carried on. Imogen came and snatched the whole lot from her and threw it away down the beach.

Meggy went and sat, all huddled, on a rock quite a long way from the others. She cried a bit more.

Helena practised cartwheels until she wanted to be the right way up again. Then she walked in the edge of the waves near to where Trevor was and looked for interesting stones. 'Stones for Stoney,' she kept saying to herself. 'Stoney's stones.'

CHAPTER ELEVEN

When It Rained

The sun failed them the next day. Helena woke up to an orchestra of rain whistling and thumping outside her window. She didn't realize at first that this would be a problem. The rehearsal today was in the village hall, not on the beach.

Trevor was having cereal poured into his dish for him. It was a new variety which he had never seen before.

'It's like little wheels, Mummy,' he said. 'Are you sure little boys can eat little wheels?'

'Yes, of course, darling,' said his mother. 'The little wheels are made of bran so they're very healthy little wheels,' and she dumped big heaps of white sugar on them.

'Now milk, Mummy, now milk!' urged Trevor and on went the milk.

'Good morning, Helena!' cried Christine when she realized she had come in.

'I'm eating little wheels, Helena!' said Trevor with the spoon in his mouth. 'Do you want some?' And he thrust his dish towards her, spilling milk in little, white pools in front of it.

'Trevor!' cried his mother, scandalized. 'Whatever's the matter with you? You don't usually spill things!'

'Sorry,' said Trevor but he was giggling. Then he looked directly at Helena and gave her the sweetest smile she had seen on a child ever.

She went into shock.

I'm dreaming, she thought, I'm getting fond of him.

She reached impulsively for a spoon in the drawer under the sink and dug it into Trevor's bowl.

'Helena, you're as bad as he is!' said Christine. 'Get a bowlful of your own!'

Helena winked at Trevor and put the spoon in her mouth.

'Ugh!' she cried. 'Oh, Trevor, I don't like them!'

Trevor laughed.

'Oh, just calm down both of you,' said Christine irritably. Then she turned to Helena. 'You'll have to think of some indoor things to do with Trevor today,' she said. 'Just look at the weather.' And she waved her hand dismissively at the rain behind the window.

Helena stopped chewing on her wheels. It had never occurred to her that Trevor wouldn't be allowed out in the rain.

'But . . . er . . . hasn't he any waterproofs?' she asked.

'Well, yes,' said Christine, sounding surprised and rather displeased. 'But I still don't think he should spend the day in the rain, do you?'

Helena just didn't know what to say.

'I'm sure you can think of some nice things to do indoors,' said Christine soothingly—and that appeared to be that. She and Robin started getting ready to go out.

'But . . . er . . . you won't be able to paint!' said Helena desperately. 'Won't you have to stay at home yourselves because . . . er . . . because you won't be able to paint?'

'My dear girl,' began Christine—which put Helena's teeth on edge immediately. 'You don't think we are limited to painting outdoors, do you? We'll just drive into Widding and there'll be all sorts of things to paint in the wine bar! Interesting customers and the flower arrangements and still-lives with the wine glasses and . . . '

'But will they let you splosh paint about in a public wine bar?' asked Helena. 'And where will you set up the easels?'

Christine was taken aback. She glanced at Robin. They both appeared to be embarrassed.

'Oh . . . er . . . we'll sort something out, I'm sure,' mumbled Robin and they both left the house very quickly.

Left alone with Trevor, Helena had a moment of panic. But it was only a moment. All I've got to do, she thought, is find Trevor's waterproofs and get him to Monica's. He never remembers anything after that anyway, so his parents won't know he went out in the rain. She went to the cupboard under the stairs where all the coats and boots were kept. Trevor had a blue waterproof coat with a purple lining and a hood, and purple wellingtons with blue turn-over tops. She knew because she had seen them before. But could she find them this time? No, she could not. She had another moment of panic.

'Trevor!' she said rather wildly. 'Do you know where your waterproofs are?'

'No, Helena,' he said.

He was sliding down the banisters—not something she had seen him do before.

Remembering her own liking for doing that as a child, she smiled at him—then realized a good, responsible 'older person' should probably be telling him to stop-because-it-was-dangerous. Plus the waterproofs were still missing, plus she would be late for the rehearsal. Panic, panic, panic.

Get a grip, she said to herself, using a phrase of her brother, Christopher's—not one she usually liked. All you have to do is ring Henry Mead and explain. Then she realized, with a sudden shock, that she hadn't got his number, or his address, or the numbers or addresses of anyone else in the theatre company. For the first time since she had known them, this struck her as rather odd.

She scrabbled desperately in the pile of things by the telephone, hoping to unearth a Serpenton-and-Surrounding-Area telephone directory, but there wasn't one there. She looked under the telephone table, in the bookshelf above it and then anywhere else in the house that seemed vaguely likely. Neither directory nor Trevor's waterproofs were forthcoming. Then she started dashing round all the unlikely places (she even looked in the bathroom and the cupboard under the stairs) but still didn't find the treasures. They would have been more welcome than silver and gold. Then she got a bit diverted and wondered if any of Monica's sea serpent stories included pirate wreckage and treasure chests.

She brought herself up short: no, no, don't waste more time, she said out loud, just keep looking.

Then there was a knock on the door. In her already nervous state, she almost screamed. She froze, Trevor froze. She was at the bottom of the stairs, he at the top. Then:

'Are you going to answer it or shall I?' said Trevor cheerfully and slid down the banisters again.

Helena opened the door.

Standing outside was a person in a long gabardine mackintosh, a large, black sou'wester and little short wellingtons. (Helena had often wondered why so many older women wore small wellingtons instead of proper, long ones.) Even the woman's walking cane had its carved head covered in a plastic bag neatly tied at the neck with green string. An old, battered leather satchel was slung over her shoulder.

'Monica,' said Helena faintly—and then, 'I mean, Miss Blaze.'

She was never sure which mode of address she should use for this woman.

'Good morning, Miss Helena Woodvine,' said Monica, saying the whole of Helena's name as if she were still trying it out. Helena, for some reason, was reminded of the formal laying-out of names in Victorian theatre programmes. She had seen them in museums. Of course, she had also fantasized about her own name being in a modern one.

There was a pause before Monica continued with, 'A very wet day.'

'Er . . . yes,' said Helena.

'May I come in?'

'Oh yes, yes of course.'

Miss Blaze stepped into the hall, put her leather bag down, and removed her sou'wester. She adjusted one or two strands of her hair, then looked archly at Helena.

'I thought you might not get your charge to my house today,' she said. 'Parents are so odd about children and the rain.' She frowned.

'Yes,' said Helena. 'I thought if I could just get him into his waterproofs, then I'd be all right but . . . '

'But he refused to put them on?' suggested Monica.

'Oh no! He's not like that any more . . . '

Monica raised her eyebrows slightly and half-smiled.

'I just can't find them.'

'Well, leave him with me,' said Monica. 'You get to your rehearsal.'

Helena stared at her.

'Well, run along then!' snapped Miss Blaze. 'Or can't you find your waterproofs either?'

Helena didn't know whether to laugh or cry.

'Oh yes, I know where mine are,' she said.

'Well get them on, then!'

Helena moved to the cupboard under the stairs so fast, she almost fell over.

Her waterproof jacket was green and reached her knees. She pulled it on and turned, rustling, to Monica.

'Thank you very much,' she said simply.

Monica inclined her head in acknowledgement. Then her brown, almond eyes started boring into Helena's which made her long to be away.

'I'd better go,' she said and opened the front door in a rush of rippling green.

'You look like the sea serpent like that,' said Monica—and the sudden dreamy tone her voice had taken on made Helena turn round again and stare.

This time, the eyes weren't looking at her but straight over her.

I bet she's got the sea in her head, thought Helena; the sea and a green serpent in it.

She left for the village hall.

In one of the scenes involving the four girls, Imogen had to flourish a newspaper at Helena. Today she had one with her so she didn't have to mime, but it must have been an old one because it blew a storm of dust into Helena's face. It didn't make her sneeze, but some of it did get trapped behind her right contact lens.

Helena cupped her hand under her eye and took it out at once.

'What are you doing?' said Julia curiously.

Helena looked at her, her eye watering like mad.

'Taking my lens out.'

'Your what?'

'My contact lens.'

There was a pause.

'May I see it?' said another voice. It was the man who played the lover—the one who wore glasses with very thick lenses.

Helena held her palm out flat and he gazed down at the tiny, translucent object in the middle of it.

He didn't say anything for a minute. Then:

'So are they instead of glasses, then?'

'Well, yes. Haven't you seen any before?' asked Helena incredulously.

He didn't reply, but shifted rather uneasily.

Once again, Helena felt doubt and panic trying to take her over. Once again, she had to push away the ideas she was getting about these people.

Think about Stoney Vale, think of Stoney, she said to herself, gritting her teeth. Never had there been a part she wanted to play more.

'Now come along, come along,' said Henry Mead, obviously trying to get things back to what he called normal. 'Let's do this scene.'

'I just need to wash . . . er . . . this thing,' said Helena, not daring to say 'contact lens' again as it seemed to cause a minor sensation.

She walked to the toilet at the back of the hall, feeling as if about fifteen pairs of eyes were charting her.

She disappeared into it as if it were a sacred refuge. The cool whiteness of the sink and the toilet bowl greeted her like statues of Greek gods.

She rinsed her lens under the cold tap, then consulted the mirror above the sink to put it back in her eye.

When she looked, she had a shock.

You've been stupid, she said to herself. Why didn't you see it before?

The eyes that were staring back at her were large and brown and almond-shaped.

Like someone else's.

Monica's.

Hers reminded you of your own, she said, not anyone else's.

She returned to the rehearsal still in a state of shock.

What was more, she still hadn't recovered before the next strange thing happened. This was at the end when people were saying goodbye. Helena was talking to Meggy and it occurred to her to ask for her phone number in case something like the delay this morning happened again.

Meggy was dumbfounded. She looked wildly around as if to seek assistance from someone, but all the others were deep in conversations of their own. Helena stared at her in surprise.

'Don't give it me if you don't want to,' she said, 'but I thought it would be nice if we could contact each other outside rehearsal time. We might want to go to the pictures or something—and I don't even know where you live!'

Meggy clasped Helena's hands.

'I'd love to go to the pictures with you!' she said. 'But I can't. I wish I could but I can't. I just can't.' And she covered her face with her hands.

'But . . . but why can't you?' asked Helena, very startled at the turn things were taking. Wasn't it perfectly normal for friends to exchange phone numbers?

'What's the matter, Helena?' asked a sudden cool voice and there was Imogen hovering over them.

'Well, it's not me,' said Helena. 'It's Meggy.'

Meggy by this time was shaking with sobs.

'Oh come on, Meggy, pull yourself together!' said Imogen, and then she turned to Helena and said, 'What have you done to her?'

'I haven't done anything to her!' cried Helena indignantly. 'I just asked for her phone number, that was all!'

'Meggy isn't on the phone,' said Imogen smoothly.

Meggy sobbed even louder.

Helena put her key in the lock that afternoon, feeling subdued and disturbed. She went to the door of the living room and opened it a crack. It creaked a bit but neither of the people in the room took any notice. She pushed it a bit wider, gasped in astonishment and opened it as wide as it would go. The whole room seemed to be full of serpents— little, paper ones all over the table and round the picture frames and hanging from the light fitting. Some were made of drawing paper and some with newspaper. Presumably, Monica had brought all that with her in the leather satchel. She and Trevor were both sitting at the table. Trevor's hands were moving busily with paper and scissors but his eyes were glazed. He had a smile on his face.

'Hello, Trevor,' said Helena experimentally, but he gave no indication that he knew she was there. He cut out a serpent, handed it to Monica without looking at her and started on another one.

'Good afternoon, Helena,' said Monica Blaze pleasantly. It was nice to hear her speak like that without the usual hint of hostility.

'Good afternoon,' said Helena, trying to avoid her eyes. She didn't want to face them now, knowing they were uncannily like hers. It was frightening. 'Have you been making sea serpents all this time?'

'Yes,' said Monica. 'It has been most enjoyable. And the rain has stopped as well.'

'Yes—a few minutes ago,' said Helena. She started pulling her waterproof off. Monica went to the cupboard under the stairs and retrieved her gabardine mackintosh and sou'wester. She put the gabardine on but folded the sou'wester neatly to put in her pocket. 'Shan't be needing that now the rain has stopped.' Just as she was completely ready to go with her cane in her hand and her short wellingtons on her feet and her satchel over her shoulder, she turned to Helena, who was half in and half out of her green waterproof, and said, 'How was the rehearsal today?' The words came out in a bit of a rush as if part of her didn't really want to know but the rest of her wanted to know desperately. This was back to her more familiar manner—half eager, half hostile. Helena's heart sank a little.

'It was all right,' she said, struggling with a green sleeve. 'But my contact——' She stopped herself because talking about contact lenses was mentioning eyes again. 'But . . . but afterwards I asked somebody for her phone number and she was all strange about it. It turned out that she wasn't on the phone at all, but she didn't say that. She just went all funny and started crying.'

'Who was that?' asked Monica sharply.

Helena looked at her, slightly taken aback.

'Who was it?' said Monica again.

'Er . . . it was a girl called Meggy Johnson.'

'Oh, Meggy!' said Monica and looked rather scornful. 'She always was such a little cry-baby!'

'Do you know her, then?' asked Helena.

'I know everyone in the theatre company,' said Monica.

Helena stopped struggling with her waterproof. For one overwhelming moment, she nearly blurted out all her fears:

'Oh, Monica,' she would have cried. 'I'm not sure about that theatre company! I think they might be——'

But as usual, the thought of Stoney Vale came tumbling into her head—and the words died on her tongue before they hit the air. She did want to be Stoney Vale so much, she just did. Maybe it was taking her over?

She stared helplessly at Monica.

Monica raised her eyebrows, then suddenly walked back into the living room.

'I must take some of these for the scrap-book,' she said and gathered three or four of the paper serpents from where they were hanging over the furniture. The ones she chose were the newspaper ones, not the plain. She placed them carefully in the satchel and then went back into the hall, opened the front door and went out. Helena stayed watching her, the green jacket hanging all askew. A little way down the road, Monica stopped and turned round.

'Do you think you'll be ready for the twelfth?' she asked.

'The twelfth?' said Helena. 'Is that when we do the first performance? No one's told me that.'

'Yes, it would have to be the same day,' said Monica half to herself.

'The same day as what?'

'Oh . . . er . . . the same day as . . . as . . . they usually do summer plays in Serpenton.' And Monica went home.

Helena finally got out of her waterproof and hung it over the stair-post. She went back into the living room to investigate Trevor. The glaze had left his eyes but he was still joyfully cutting out sea serpents.

'Did you have a nice day?' asked Helena.

'Oh yes,' said Trevor. He finished his serpent, hung it carefully over the back of a chair and then pushed the paper and scissors to one side. 'There's lots and lots of those things, aren't there, Helena?' he said. 'Squiggling and wriggling all over the place!'

'Yes,' said Helena. 'There are. You and Monica made them.'

'Was it Monica?' he said hazily. 'Who's Monica? Wasn't it you who made them? And me. I did too.'

Then he started whirling like a little dervish.

'Everywhere, everywhere,' he chanted. 'Whirly things. Whirly-curly, hurdy-gurdy!'

Helena laughed.

Suddenly, he sank down, exhausted.

There was a pause.

'Please can I watch television now?' he asked pleasantly.

'Yes, of course you can,' said Helena—and, to her amazement, she almost added 'darling'. She had to bite her tongue to stop herself. 'Ouch!' she cried as a result.

Trevor turned the television on, and sprawled rather engagingly in an armchair in front of it.

About half an hour later, Helena jumped up in alarm and flew into the hall. She snatched her waterproof off the stair-post and bundled it into the cupboard under the stairs. She was just closing the door on the evidence when Robin and Christine arrived home. A couple of seconds earlier and they would have seen that Helena had gone out in the rain after all. And of course they would have assumed that she had taken Trevor with her. There would have been all hell to answer for. Helena went weak at the knees just with the thought.

However, Christine was not much better pleased to see the whole of the living room writhing with paper serpents.

'Need you have made quite so many, dears?' she asked. 'And what are they, anyway?'

'Oh . . . just patterns,' said Trevor vaguely. A stuffed cat was speaking on the television and Trevor was sure that its message was meant entirely for him.

'They're not just patterns,' said Helena, greatly daring. 'They're sea serpents.'

'There's no such thing,' said Trevor, nodding at the cat to show he had understood its message.

'Oh, Helena!' said Christine. 'The ideas you get!' She and Robin both laughed.

'Did you do any painting in the wine bar?' asked Helena.

'Don't be silly, dear,' said Christine, laughing again. 'How could we set up our easels in a public wine bar?'

Chapter Twelve

A Bombshell

The next morning at breakfast as Trevor and Helena were eating wheels with milk and Robin and Christine were eating toast with marmalade, the phone rang. Christine went to answer it and they heard her shrieking, 'Oh, hello! How lovely to hear from you!' Quite a long time afterwards she came back in and said, 'It was your mummy, Helena, dear.'

'I don't call her "Mummy",' said Helena furiously.

'Don't you?' said Trevor with interest. 'Shall I stop calling you Mummy, Mummy?'

Christine frowned, but before she could answer, he had bounced back in with, 'What could I call her instead, Helena?'

Helena was instantly thronged with so many ideas (most of them not polite) that she choked on her breakfast-wheels.

Trevor looked thoughtfully ahead of him, his spoon cocked at an inspiring angle in the air.

Even his mother was poised now, waiting for his answer, her brows gathered.

'Let me see, let me see,' said Trevor tantalizingly.

Helena started to giggle, Christine glowered at her and Trevor came up with his answer:

'Mrs Fish-Face,' he said.

There was a pause.

'Helena, that's your fault!' exploded Christine. 'Trevor was never like this before he met you!'

Helena banged her spoon down on the table.

'But you asked me to come away with you!' she cried. 'No . . . you didn't ask, you press-ganged me—you and my mother!'

'Ah yes, your mother,' said Christine, calming down a little. 'She rang. She rang a few minutes ago.'

'So you said,' said Helena shortly. 'What did she want? Why didn't she speak to me?'

'Well, she was going to,' said Christine. 'But then we both got a bit carried away and she decided she'd better not make her phone bill even worse!' And she tinkled with feminine laughter. 'But don't worry,' she continued. 'You're going to see her tomorrow. It's all arranged!'

'What?' said Helena, making a sudden nervous movement that caused the milk to shudder in her dish. 'Do you mean she's coming here?'

'Yes, dear,' said Christine. 'She wants to spend the whole day with you. Isn't that nice?'

'What about Trevor?' said Helena at once.

'Oh, we'll take him with us. We won't mind just for one day. And after all, our new friends are longing to meet him, aren't they, Robin?'

'Yes,' said Robin.

Trevor looked rather disgruntled.

'What time is she getting here?' Helena almost whispered.

'Her train gets in at 9.15. You'd like to meet it, wouldn't you? Then you must bring her back here and we'll all have coffee together, before Robin and I go off painting. I had decided anyway it was time you had some time off from looking after Trevor.' (Ha, ha, thought Helena.)

She explained the disaster to Monica later and was amazed at her response:

'That's no problem,' she said shortly.

'Why isn't it?' asked Helena. 'I'll have to spend the whole day with her and not go to the rehearsal!'

'You won't be spending the whole day with her and you will be at the rehearsal,' corrected Monica. 'She can come here and I'll . . . tell her about the serpent like Trevor.'

She said it completely dead-pan as if she were saying, 'I'll take her shopping.'

'But . . . but we can't!' cried Helena. 'Not my mother!'

'Why not?'

'Because . . . well . . . because she's an adult!'

'The sea serpent has entertained many different people in his time,' said Monica with dignity. 'He is by no means limited to children.'

'I'm sorry,' said Helena blankly.

Later still, when she told Henry about the visit, he made an unexpected announcement to the whole company:

'The rehearsal will begin later tomorrow and will probably go on a little later as well. Can you all be here by one, please?'

Then he spoke to Helena again.

'That's to give you some time with your mother before she goes to Monica's. You'd like that, wouldn't you? After all, you haven't seen her for a few days, have you?' And he looked at her in a 'parenty' way which she had never seen him do before. But after all, he was one himself.

Helena went crimson.

'Just a couple of hours would be all right,' she mumbled guiltily.

CHAPTER THIRTEEN

The Bombshell Dealt With

The train bearing Helena's mother was thirteen minutes late. Helena was waiting at the barrier. She nearly had a fit when she finally saw her mother. Mrs Woodvine was wearing a pink summer dress—and a hat. It was the hat that upset Helena. It was basically a straw one which would have been all right in itself but it had a cluster of bright imitation cherries attached to it. Helena wanted to die.

'Mum!' she hissed. 'You don't usually wear hats—not if it isn't a wedding or anything.'

'I thought it would be just the thing for the seaside!' said her mother gaily, patting the top of it.

'But why did you have to get one with cherries on it? It wouldn't be so bad if they were real ones but—'

'Don't be silly, dear,' said Mrs Woodvine. 'The cherries make it.' Then she kissed her daughter and they walked away. Three seagulls were wheeling overhead to herald the arrival. The sun shone down on the imitation cherries.

'Are you going to show me around the village, Helena?' asked her mother.

Helena worked out a plan for the morning in her head. She would take her mother the long way round the village to show it to her; get back to the cottage to gush with the Mellings for a while and then deliver her to Monica. She hastily re-phrased that last thought. It sounded like delivering her to the executioners. Take her to meet Monica would do instead.

They plunged into the little web of narrow, winding streets. Helena's mother suddenly turned her head sharply.

'Helena, did you see . . .' she said—and then turned her head the other way. 'I thought there was . . . oh, I'm not sure.'

'It's like that here,' said Helena, and was surprised at how complacently the words came out of her mouth: she was obviously used to the place now. 'You're never quite sure whether things are really here or not.'

'Oh, darling, don't be silly!' said her mother with just the faintest tinge of panic in her voice. She looked round about her. 'It's . . . it's very pretty,' she said rather desperately.

'Oh yes,' said Helena. 'The cottages are nice.'

They turned into the cobbled street where Mrs Fields's shop was.

'Is this the only shop there is?' asked her mother in amazement.

'I've never thought about it,' said Helena. 'Yes, I suppose it is.'

Opposite the shop was a small post box, the sort that is let into the wall—and it stood out much more than a post box usually would because it was a little bit of bright red among all the grey. There were colours in the front of Mrs Fields's shop too—the lettering was in green and there were small panes of blue and green glass at the top and bottom of the big window—and in the window part of the door. For the first time, Helena realized that these very slight glimmers of colour made this particular street quite outstanding in Serpenton. The road opposite the sea would be similar because of the sign swinging outside the pub—the picture of the sea serpent. It was very faded so the painted image of the serpent was probably nothing like as green as the one in Monica's head, but still it stood out in clear relief to the grey houses on either side of it.

Mrs Woodvine didn't seem particularly interested in the

shop but she was drawn to the post box as if to a red oasis. She stood looking at it as if she wanted to reassure herself with something ordinary in this strange place.

'It's only a post box, Mum!' said Helena impatiently.

'It's a particularly nice one, isn't it?' said her mother.

'Yes, yes,' said Helena, thinking about time passing—and the deed that was yet to be done. 'Come on.'

They turned into another street. Helena tripped suddenly over a trailing shoe lace and went down on one knee to tie it again. While she was near to the ground, she noticed little scraps of plant-life sprouting up between the paving stones and they seemed much greener and more significant than they would in any other village, like the post box seemed much redder. The rest of the place was shifting, dreaming grey—not un-attractive but always with that air of waiting. Dozing and waiting. Waiting for what?

'Where's the church?' asked her mother suddenly.

'What church?'

'There must be a church! All these places have one. I'd like to look round it.'

She always liked to look at churches.

Helena felt a chill between her shoulder-blades.

'There isn't one,' she said, realizing this information for the first time herself.

'Oh, Helena, there must be! Maybe you just haven't found it yet.'

'No,' said Helena. 'There isn't one.'

She and her mother looked at each other. Very odd really: they never went to church services except at Christmas because they liked carols but both of them felt an unknown fear at there simply not being one.

'Where do you suppose they bury their dead?' asked Helena fearfully.

'Oh, there'll be somewhere!' cried her mother, probably trying to be reassuring but sounding merely panicky. 'You know, somewhere consecrated.'

'But consecrated to what?'

'Oh, Helena, Helena!'

A long silence.

'Time to go to the Mellings'!' said Helena. 'Now. Let's go now!'

Her mother's voice wobbled with relief.

'Yes, I'm dying for a cup of coffee!' And then they both took in she had used the word 'dying' and giggled very nervously.

All the way to the Mellings', Helena kept wondering about the dead of Serpenton. Did they get thrown out to sea for the 'serpent' to deal with? Did tradition overshadow belief?

As soon as Trevor saw Mrs Woodvine, he said, 'Hello. That's a very funny hat!'

'Trevor!' said his mother.

'Oh,' said Mrs Woodvine, sounding rather worried. 'I don't think it's meant to be funny, Trevor, dear.'

'Well it is, you know,' said Trevor with perfect politeness. 'It's like a clown's hat. Do those cherries spurt out water?'

There was a pause.

Helena was trying not to laugh.

With an abrupt movement not typical of her, Mrs Woodvine removed her hat.

'Shouldn't wear this indoors!' she said, trying to make light of it.

Mrs Melling took it off her—she almost snatched it. But then she placed it gently and reverently on a little table.

With the controversial object removed, both the mothers seemed more relaxed.

The dining room table was laid out with coffee and cream and sugar and scones. The scones were the sort that didn't have any currants in which made Helena feel slightly bored. Everyone sat round the table.

The coffee party dragged on interminably. Helena was reduced to making pyramids with a spoon in the sugar. It was fine, brown sugar like a little bowl of sand. It made her think of the beach.

Trevor started doing it too. Their spoons clashed which made their eyes meet and they grinned at each other. It was a very companionable moment.

'Helena, you're being a very bad example!' cried her mother suddenly—and Helena jumped so violently that some of the sugar flew out of the dish. Trevor promptly flicked some out with his spoon.

'Trevor!' cried Christine. 'Whatever's the matter with you?'

'We ought to go,' said Robin hurriedly and, at last, the three Mellings took their leave. Robin and Christine were carrying their painting things and Trevor was handed a small sketch book and some wax crayons which made Helena grin. Little did they know that this was a version of Trevor's usual image for part of the day. The things were new but he didn't seem very impressed. Maybe at the back of his mind, there did lurk a memory of the beautiful green and gold scrapbook and the elegant pencils that Monica gave him—although he didn't act as if he remembered anything about them.

'I do much better things with Helena!' he proclaimed.

'Yes,' said Christine rather sarcastically. She was probably thinking of the paper serpents that had littered her living room so inconveniently.

A pause and then:

'Have a wonderful day's painting!' gushed Mrs Woodvine and she stood at the window to watch them get into the car. Her daughter remained sitting at the table.

Mrs Woodvine waved until they were out of sight and then Helena sprang up and said, 'Right, come on, Mum, I've got a friend I want you to meet.'

To her own surprise, referring to Monica as a 'friend' came out very swiftly and easily.

And yet the woman was so difficult!

And old. Older than Helena's mother!

'A friend,' said her mother. 'How have you found time to make a friend if you've been playing with Trevor?'

Helena didn't answer.

'Does Trevor like her too?' her mother persisted.

'How do you know it's a "her"?' snapped Helena at once. 'It might be a "him".' And she peered curiously at her mother to see if the usual reaction was registering. And it was. Or so it seemed to Helena. Her mother was funny about men. Helena was convinced that she had only married her father because she was desperate to have children. She had had James and Christopher very quickly (they were twins) then, as she put it, 'he had made her wait' for four years before she had Helena. She had her daughter and that was it then—she left him. This was the story that Helena had gathered.

There was a pause.

'It's a "her",' said Helena. 'And she's quite old. Older than you.'

Mrs Woodvine raised her eyebrows in surprise.

'And do you get on with her?' she asked rather plaintively which sent a pang through Helena's heart which she instantly suppressed.

'Sort of,' she replied shortly.

On the way to Monica's house, Mrs Woodvine made a remark:

'Do you still think you want to be an actress?' she asked.

'Of course,' said Helena.

What a stupid question!

Her mother gnawed her lip for a moment, but then asked something else:

'Do you always wear those shorts?' she asked.

This had more effect. Helena stopped in her tracks.

'Why?' she asked suspiciously. 'What's wrong with them?'

She hated personal remarks about clothes. She was wearing longish green shorts with turn-ups and a white T-shirt. She was very fond of both garments.

'I was just wondering if you would like a nice new dress to wear. I could make you one.'

Helena stared at her.

'Well, you know, I'd like one,' she said carefully. 'I want one with buttons down the front and short sleeves like all my friends have got.' She put a lot of emphasis on the 'all'.

There was a pause . . .

'Please,' she added, feeling strangely childlike.

Her mother sighed.

'It is funny how those awful things have come back in fashion,' she said. 'I think if I see girls wearing them, I imagine I'm back in my cot when I was a baby and my sisters are swooshing past with them on and I can hear the bombs landing and I'm terrified.'

Helena had never heard her mother talk like this before. It was alarming, but she was touched somehow. Her own voice softened.

'But wouldn't you have been in an air-raid shelter?' she asked. 'You wouldn't have been in a cot in a room when there was an air raid.'

'I'm not sure my parents always bothered going to it,' her mother answered. 'It got like that, you know. People got to the stage when they thought "If we die, we die. So what?"'

Helena just didn't know what to say to that.

They walked in silence for a few minutes.

Then, after an inward struggle that was obvious to Helena too, her mother said, 'I'll see what I can do about a dress.'

'Thank you, Mum,' said Helena rather quietly.

They were very nearly at Monica's house and the road was starting to steepen. Mrs Woodvine then made a remark about Trevor.

'He's changed, Helena,' she said. 'I used to think he was such a nice, polite little boy but now . . . ' she tailed off.

'Yes?' asked Helena, grinning.

'Well, don't you think he's gone a bit cheeky?'

'Oh, but I like him much better!' cried Helena. 'He wasn't normal before.'

There was a pause. They were just reaching Monica's gate. The strange, iron window-box was twisting itself into their vision.

'Helena,' said her mother and she sounded rather strained. 'What have you been doing with him?'

Everything seemed to go dead silent. Helena felt her heart beat loudly and hollowly three times before the door of the cottage suddenly opened and Monica was there.

'Hello,' said Monica. 'You must be Helena's mother.'

'Er . . . yes,' said Mrs Woodvine but for some reason she wasn't looking at her. She was staring fixedly at the window-box.

'It's a curiosity, isn't it?' said Monica softly.

'Yes,' said Helena's mother in a dreamy, far-away voice. 'Where did you get it?'

'Someone gave it to me.'

A pause.

'Would you like to come in?'

Mrs Woodvine went in and stayed in. Helena went to the rehearsal.

It seemed like only a couple of seconds later, that she was plunged into the rehearsal as if her mother were miles away.

Today, she found that Monica Blaze was right. The first performance was to be on the twelfth of August, which was a week away. They had already been rehearsing for a week, but it felt a lot longer. Helena couldn't help thinking that these particular two rehearsal weeks were for her benefit. Everyone else had seemed to be more or less ready before she even joined the company. It wasn't that they were all brilliant actors and actresses, but they had all known their lines and their moves and were probably as ready as they would ever be. Not for the first time, Helena wondered why the original 'Stoney Vale' had dropped out—and how long had been the gap between losing her and finding herself. She had tried asking about it but, like a lot of other things she had approached in conversation, nobody really answered her properly and they always looked awkward. It usually ended with Imogen making some smooth comment that shut everyone up immediately.

To Helena's surprise and disappointment, she also discovered today that the first performance on the twelfth was to be the only one. Never in her life had she been in a play that had lasted for less than three nights.

'One will be quite enough,' said Henry quietly.

'Yes, quite enough!' echoed most of the others in chorus and they looked at each other very significantly. Their eyes shone.

Helena started up again.

'I've just thought of something! What's happening about the costumes? When will—'

'What are you worrying about?' said Imogen. 'They're all

in there,' and she waved her hand at a door to the left of the platform.

'They're all ready,' said Meggy. 'All hanging on hooks.'

'But what about mine?' said Helena.

'Yours is in there,' said Imogen. 'Don't worry.'

'Can I have a look?' said Helena eagerly and got up.

'No!' said Julia and grabbed her arm. 'It . . . er . . . it wouldn't be good luck,' she said, seeing the surprise on Helena's face. 'Not before the day of the dress rehearsal.'

'The set is in the room on the other side,' said Imogen. 'In case you're wondering about that too.'

'Everything was ready before you even joined the company,' said Julia and laughed nervously.

Helena gave her a nervous look in return—and then Miss Smith saw fit to make a contribution:

'Talking of costume,' she said in her oddly ungenerous voice, 'I've been wondering why you wear shorts like a boy. Haven't you got any dresses?'

The comment, reminiscent of her mother's, made Helena swiftly forget any resolution to put up gracefully with Miss Smith. She spun round and was about to make some explosive, offended retort when Imogen dealt with it for her. Imogen's methods were much calmer than Helena's.

'Don't be silly, Miss Smith,' she said. 'It wouldn't be very practical to rehearse Stoney Vale in a dress, now would it?'

'No, she'd show her knickers all the time when she was doing handstands!' said Julia.

'Thank you, Julia,' said Imogen.

Miss Smith was so overcome with 'knickers' being said to her in public that she pursed her mouth up and could think of nothing more to say. Helena realized once again how heartily she disliked Miss Smith. This time, she was so stung by her that she had to say something to someone else.

'Meggy,' she whispered when the rehearsal had started

again, 'why does Miss Smith keep coming to rehearsals? She doesn't do anything.'

Meggy stared at her in surprise.

'Don't you know?' she said.

'No.'

'Well, she wrote the play.'

'What?'

Helena felt as if someone had just pushed her very hard. She couldn't say anything for several seconds.

'Are you sure?' she said at last.

'Of course I'm sure,' said Meggy.

Helena stared at Miss Smith then and couldn't look away. How could such a miserable person have produced such a lovely play?

Somehow she had. Somehow there were things in her head that didn't come out in her everyday personality, but blazed into startling life on paper.

Just before the end of the rehearsal, Miss Smith spoke to Helena again. She said, 'Pass me that pen on the piano, Helen.'

Helena was still so overcome by what she had learnt that she passed it to her in a trance—not seeming to notice that Miss Smith hadn't said 'please' or that she had got her name wrong yet again.

When she arrived back at Monica's house, she found the front door open and her mother sitting on a chair outside. Her hair was brushing the iron window-box like Monica's had that time and she was reading a magazine. When she heard Helena approaching, she looked up and Helena gasped at the expression on her face. It wasn't quite like Trevor's was on these occasions; it didn't shine with joy—but it wasn't far off being like that. Maybe it took longer if you were older.

And she smiled.

Helena smiled back.

Then, through the open front door, she saw Monica walk down the hallway with a tray of tea things.

'Hello,' said Monica to them both. 'Did you have a nice time?'

'Oh yes,' said Mrs Woodvine at once. 'We went to the beach.'

Helena was about to go into 'But you weren't there, Mum,' when she received a warning look from Monica.

Then they grinned at each other—and it was 'grinning', not polite little smiles.

'Come into the parlour,' said Monica then and they both obeyed. Somehow it seemed suitable that Monica should say 'parlour', not 'sitting room'.

Something happened in the 'parlour'. They were just raising their tea-cups to their lips, when a photograph frame on the mantelpiece fell over.

'What made that happen?' cried Helena. She was never very far from nervousness these days.

'It's all right, dear,' said her mother placidly and got up to pick it up again.

'Something's falling out of it,' she said.

The displayed photograph was still firmly in the frame but another one was slipping out from behind it. Helena's mother didn't take it out properly and gawp at it (she was far too polite for that) but she did glance at it in passing and then cried out in surprise.

'Helena, why were you asking me for one of those dresses? It looks as if you've already got one!'

'What?' said Helena blankly. 'What are you talking about?'

Monica got up abruptly—then seemed to change her mind and sat down again. She heaved a sigh.

'Miss Blaze has got this photograph of you with it on!'

'Don't be so silly!' cried Helena who had now got up to

104

take a look at it. 'How can it be a photograph of me? It's an old black and white one. You can see it's all faded and frayed.'

'Oh . . . of course,' said her mother faintly. 'How ridiculous of me!'

There was a pause.

'Oh . . . but, Helena,' she added in a daze, 'it is so like you! It's uncanny!'

Helena went to take the photograph herself to get a proper look. But another hand reached over and stopped her. Monica's.

'See it another time,' she said quietly.

And then Helena found herself going into a state of panic which she was barely able to control. She wanted to stand there and blurt out everything she felt about the theatre company and Serpenton and wanting to be an actress and her mother and her brothers and the father she seldom saw . . .

Monica must have realized something was up because she immediately went into an iron command. She cleared the tea things away at lightning speed and retrieved Mrs Woodvine's hat ready to leave and practically pushed both her and Helena out of the front door. Mrs Woodvine was in a sort of gushing haze, saying what a nice time she had had and 'thank you very much' . . .

Helena by now was grim and silent, not trusting herself to speak. She marched her mother to the station.

Then, just as they reached the platform, Mrs Woodvine turned to Helena and her face was all lit up.

'I've got a surprise for you,' she said. 'You're going to have two more visitors!'

Helena's face dropped. She was reminded of Scrooge in *A Christmas Carol* being told by Jacob Marley that his ordeal wasn't over and he would be seeing more ghosts.

'Who?' she said huskily.

'Oh, you silly girl, who do you think?' laughed Mrs Woodvine. 'The family, of course! Christopher can come the day after tomorrow and James two days after that! Isn't that nice? It's a pity they can't both come on the same day, of course, but never mind.'

'What about Dad?' asked Helena sarcastically. 'Have you fixed it for him to come too?'

Her mother pretended she hadn't heard that.

How Helena wished that she would stop trying to convince herself that her three children loved each other much more than they loved anyone else. Helena did get on quite well with James but she hardly knew him really—and Christopher she positively disliked. How on earth had her mother persuaded him to come? She must have promised him something 'mega' (as he would say) for his birthday or something.

The only thing that relieved the pain of this announcement was her realization that the hideous plastic cherries on her mother's hat had mysteriously disappeared . . .

After Mrs Woodvine had gone, Helena went rushing back to Monica's.

'Come in,' said Monica at once when she saw her pale and trembling state. 'I thought you'd come back tonight.'

'Oh, Monica,' said Helena. 'I don't know what to do! I keep having such terrifying thoughts about the theatre company! I keep thinking they might be gho—'

To her astonishment, she felt Monica's hand go over her mouth to stop her saying any more. She abruptly obeyed. Monica took her hand away at once.

'Sorry,' said Monica awkwardly.

A wicker chair creaked in a corner and they both jumped—even Monica, who must have been used to it.

'Listen,' said Monica, 'I know it's odd, Helena, and there's

106

things you don't understand, but . . . well, can you trust me?'

'Yes,' said Helena at once and without a qualm.

'Just carry on with it then! Do the play, don't ask questions. If you have any doubts, squash them. If you have any fears, ignore them. It's the right thing to do, I promise you. Just do it, do it!'

Helena stared at her. She sounded like a Catholic priest she had once heard in a play. The words rang in her ears. Clamorous and glamorous both at the same time.

But then Monica subsided. Pain shot into her face. The usual disarming conflict: helping Helena on the one hand yet apparently feeling some kind of desperate jealousy on the other.

'That photograph's of you, isn't it?' said Helena. 'The one that fell out of the frame? Do I look like you did when you were younger? Is that what startled my mum?'

Monica didn't answer.

'I'm going now,' said Helena hastily. 'Thank you very much. I'm going now. Goodnight.'

She let herself out—and ran home through the early summer evening as if it were night and frightening dark.

CHAPTER FOURTEEN

Christopher In Serpenton

Christine Melling was not amused.

'Whatever possessed you to invite your brothers to come?' she asked.

'It wasn't my idea!' said Helena indignantly. 'It was my mum's.'

'Oh!' said Christine. 'Well, you're supposed to be here to help with Trevor. That's what the pocket money's for. I'm afraid it's not convenient for us to have him when we're painting. You'll have to keep him with you on the days they come.'

Helena merely shrugged. Whoever she was stuck with was going to be delivered to Monica's anyway—and would stay there while she and Trevor went to the rehearsal—like her mother had.

However, Robin intervened. Maybe he was feeling guilty. He said that Helena was surely entitled to some days off and, so far, she had only had one the whole time she had been there—the day her mother came. So Christine reluctantly agreed that on the day Christopher came, they would take Trevor with them again.

However, no offer of giving Christopher coffee in the morning was made.

Helena met Christopher's train. He came on a later one than their mother had—and would be going back on an earlier one. As soon as she saw him, Helena knew for sure it hadn't been his own idea to come. He walked down the platform with his hands in his pockets and his head down. If there had been a Coke tin lying around, he would have kicked it. But there weren't any Coke drinkers in Serpenton. He came to the barrier, thrust his return ticket under the guard's nose, saw Helena and gave her an aggressive nod. 'Hi,' he said. Helena hated people who said 'Hi'!

'Hello,' she replied without enthusiasm and they moved off.

'What a dump!' said Christopher immediately.

'No it's not!'

Brother and sister glared at each other for two or three seconds.

'What have you got planned for me then?' asked Christopher. 'Orgies on the beach? A wild afternoon on the pier?'

'What pier?'

'Exactly!' said Christopher and moodily kicked a stone — since there wasn't a tin.

'This way,' said Helena and marched to Monica's house.

'But what's this?' cried Christopher as soon as he realized he was being taken up to the front door of an unremarkable cottage (unremarkable except for the iron window-box— but he hadn't noticed that).

'What does it look like?' said Helena sarcastically. 'It's someone's house.'

'Whose?'

'A friend of mine.'

'But . . . '

The door was opened.

To Helena's surprise, Monica seemed a bit uncertain when she looked at Christopher.

'Good morning,' she said but not with the usual hypnotic confidence.

Christopher stared coldly at her.

'Hi,' he said.

Monica glanced at Helena.

'Er . . . this is Monica Blaze,' said Helena desperately, 'and . . . ' her voice trailed off.

'Come in,' said Monica in the voice that usually pulled Trevor into the hallway.

'What for?' said Christopher. 'I thought I was here for a day at the beach. And what a beach,' he added derisively.

'Go on then,' said Monica. 'Go to the beach. Good morning.'

Helena stared at her in amazement. Was she giving up so soon?

With an abrupt shrug, Christopher turned and made off back down the sloping road.

'It wouldn't have worked with him,' said Monica.

Helena didn't question what the 'it' referred to.

'The rehearsal?' she almost whispered.

'I'm afraid you'll have to miss one,' said Monica. 'I can't help today.'

Helena stared at her in horrified disbelief.

Miss a development in the 'Stoney Vale' quest? It was unthinkable.

'I'm sorry,' said Monica more gently. 'I'll make sure Henry Mead knows you can't make it—and why. You go after your brother. Quick. Before he disappears.'

Helena looked down the road after her brother's gradually diminishing back. He was wearing a faded denim jacket. His shoulders were slightly raised and he had his hands in his pockets. He was walking neither quickly nor slowly.

Miss a rehearsal and spend the time with him. That was to be her day.

She felt very choked as she was catching him up.

They got as far as the beach without speaking, then Christopher stopped and started throwing stones into the sea. Luckily, he got interested in trying to 'skim' them across the top of the water so that kept him absorbed for about half an hour. Reluctantly, Helena had to admit that he was quite good at it, although she said nothing to him.

While he was doing that, she turned a row of cartwheels over a long patch of dried-up seaweed. It felt pleasantly crackly under her hands and feet. Then she chose a barer patch of sand and walked on her hands. There were prints from seagull feet there as well.

'It's half-past eleven,' said Christopher. 'Take me to the nearest pub—oh damn! You're too young, aren't you?'

'It doesn't matter,' said Helena.

She took him to The Sea Serpent where Robin and Christine had once been. The door was wedged open. There were four or five people in there whom Helena had never seen before. But they smiled at her as she hovered at the threshold and she smiled back. They were probably some of the people coming to see the play on the twelfth of August. Mrs Fields had said that everyone in Serpenton would come even though you never saw them at any other time.

Christopher looked up at the sign and said 'The Sea Serpent! What a stupid name for a pub!'

There was one table and one chair outside The Sea Serpent. Christopher took the chair and Helena sat on the paving stones, her back against the wall. It was very warm. Christopher drank beer and Helena had shandy, which she detested, but she didn't want to look a wimp with orange juice. They stayed there for quite a long time, Christopher getting up once to buy more beer and Helena not getting up at all. They hardly spoke a word to each other the whole time. At half-past one, Christopher went into the bar again and bought three bread rolls. He handed one to Helena and ate the other two himself. Then he went back in and came out with a packet of crisps and a packet of peanuts. He offered Helena one sample from each packet and poured the rest down his throat. He coughed on a splinter of crisp and indicated furiously that Helena was to thump him on the back to dislodge it. She did this with great relish and he glared at her. 'Not that hard!' he said when he could speak again. Then he had a pint of lemonade. Helena had the same with relief. The shandy made her shudder. She had thirteen pence left in her purse.

'Is there anywhere I can buy a Mars bar?' said Christopher as they left The Sea Serpent. She led him to Mrs Fields's shop. She and Mrs Fields exchanged greetings. They were very pleased to see each other.

'Er . . . this is my brother,' said Helena. 'Christopher, this is Mrs Fields.'

'Hello,' said Mrs Fields.

'Hi, can I have a Mars bar?' said Christopher.

Just as they were leaving the shop, an old lady came in. As soon as she saw Helena, she smiled. Somebody else to see the play, thought Helena and smiled back. That made six people in one day she had never seen before.

Christopher finished his Mars bar and threw the wrapper on the ground.

'Pick that up!' said Helena furiously.

He ignored her so she picked it up herself and stuffed it into one of his pockets. He looked as if he was about to pull it out again and throw it in her face, but then he just shrugged and carried on walking.

They went back to the beach and he did some more stone-skimming. This time, Helena had a go as well.

'Useless,' said Christopher at her first attempt—so she turned her back on him and did cartwheels until she was quite a distance away. Then she stood on her hands.

She was still upside-down when a familiar voice said, 'Hello, Helena.' She started violently (an interesting experience when you are the wrong way up) and came down in a heap.

'Sorry!' said another voice.

'What are you saying "sorry" for when it was me that startled her?' said the first voice. Imogen and Julia were standing beside her.

'Hello,' said Helena. 'What are you doing here?'

'There aren't many scenes we can do without you,' said Julia. 'So we've been let off early.'

'Is that your brother?' said Imogen suddenly, looking across at Christopher skimming stones.

'Yes.'

'He's very good-looking,' said Julia.

'Do you think so?' said Helena in surprise.

'Yes,' said Imogen decisively. 'He is.' She started walking towards him.

'Oh, Imogen what are you doing?' said Julia and giggled. She followed her sister.

Helena sat down and watched them curiously. They both went very close to him and watched him with the stones. Christopher completely ignored them. Then Julia whispered something to Imogen and Imogen pushed her impatiently away. They watched for a few more minutes and then Imogen picked up a stone and stood beside him. She flicked it into the water and it danced across for four or five bounces. Better than any of Christopher's so far. He started as if in surprise and looked about in every direction. He still didn't acknowledge Imogen. He could at least smile or say 'hi', thought Helena angrily. Julia had her hands over her mouth and her eyes were goggling.

Helena could feel the fury mounting: she wanted to ask him what he was playing at. She nearly did.

But then another thought struck her. A terrifying one.

Her brother was acting as if he simply couldn't see her friends. So maybe he couldn't. Maybe . . .

Monica's voice suddenly flashed into her head. Monica

113

in her 'Catholic preacher' voice saying, 'Don't question anything. Just do it.'

She held back from admonishing Christopher and, a moment later, he looked at his watch and strode towards her.

'It's time I went,' he said.

Helena made signs across to Imogen and Julia to say she was going to the station with Christopher. They both looked disappointed.

'What are you flapping your hands about at nothing for?' said Christopher.

Helena shuddered and didn't answer him.

'Can you find your own way back to the station?' she asked, changing her mind about accompanying him.

'Of course,' said Christopher.

'Goodbye then.'

'Goodbye,' said Christopher. 'What a weird place this is! Don't know how you stand it.'

He left.

Helena walked over to Imogen and Julia.

'I'm sorry about that,' she said.

'About what?' said Imogen.

'About him being so rude and just ignoring you.'

'It doesn't matter,' said Imogen. She seemed rather subdued, Helena thought. Surely she hadn't really liked Christopher?

'It's not his fault he can't s—' began Julia.

'Look, here comes Meggy,' said Imogen interrupting her but not quite as forcefully as usual.

'Oh, Meggy,' said Julia breathlessly. 'You've just missed Helena's brother. He's gorgeous!'

'Did he see you?' said Meggy in surprise.

Julia looked at Imogen as if waiting for her to do something, but Imogen was totally abstracted. So then Julia nudged Meggy hard, the way Imogen so often did to her. Meggy started and looked at Helena.

'Oh . . . I didn't think!'

'Didn't think what?' said Helena uneasily, not really wanting an answer.

There was an awkward pause.

'You're . . . you're quiet, Imogen,' said Meggy nervously.

'Am I?' said Imogen. 'Just thinking.'

'Helena's brother did this,' said Julia and lobbed a stone clumsily into the sea.

'No he didn't, he did this,' said Imogen and skimmed one gracefully across the waves.

'Look,' said Julia. 'There's somebody else coming.'

The other three turned and there was Monica Blaze walking down from the village. Suddenly and quite unexpectedly, she stopped dead. She appeared to be looking at them.

'What's she staring at?' said Julia and turned her back on her. She hurled another stone into the water.

'She's staring at us,' said Imogen.

'Who is she?' said Meggy.

'Don't you know?' said Helena in surprise. 'Well, I'm sure she said she knows you.'

Monica Blaze went right up to them and stopped.

'Can we help you?' said Imogen.

'You don't know who I am, do you?'

Imogen, Julia, and Meggy stared at her.

'But I don't understand,' began Helena. 'I thought . . . '

'You look . . . I mean . . . I think you might be . . .' said Julia—but Imogen said, 'I know who you are. You're Monica.'

Meggy gave a cry and backed away.

'Oh come on, Megan!' exclaimed Monica. 'All right, so I'm much older now! It happens to us all, you know.' She faltered. 'Well, most of us anyway.'

They all looked uneasy—even Imogen.

'Anyway, how is your new Stoney Vale?' asked Monica. There was a dead silence and Helena felt terribly embarrassed.

'She's good, she's good!' cried Meggy hysterically. 'She's very, very—'

'Shut up, Meggy!' hissed Imogen. 'Yes, she's good,' she said to Monica. 'She plays it differently to . . . to . . . '

'To how it was played before,' finished Monica.

'It was good then as well,' said Imogen quietly.

'Are you coming to see it?' blurted out Julia.

Imogen glared at her—but Monica answered the question.

'Of course I am!' she cried indignantly. 'Did you think I wouldn't?'

Julia went red.

'Of course, I'm not sure how I'll feel afterwards,' said Monica and she didn't sound indignant any more—just sad.

There was another pause.

'Are you married, Monica?' asked Imogen suddenly.

'No,' said Monica.

Imogen swung round unexpectedly on Helena then.

'Have you ever fallen in love?' she asked rather brusquely.

'Er . . . not really,' said Helena. 'Not yet.'

'But you will,' said Imogen. 'You will one day. And then another day with someone else. And then again with someone else.'

'Er . . . probably,' said Helena, totally bewildered at the turn things had taken.

'Do you remember Michael Green?' said Imogen to Monica.

'Yes,' said Monica.

'He looked a bit like Helena's brother.'

'No he didn't, Imogen!' exclaimed Julia.

'I think he did,' said Imogen in the sort of voice that no one contradicts.

'Who's Michael Green?' whispered Helena to Meggy.

'A boy Imogen used to like,' Meggy whispered back.

'Doesn't she see him any more?'

Meggy just looked at her.

What that wordless reply was supposed to mean, Helena had no idea.

The five of them stood there awkwardly for a few seconds.

'Right, I must go,' said Monica. Meggy must have looked relieved or something because she then said, 'You'll have to get used to people looking older, you know, Megan.'

'Yes,' whispered Meggy.

Monica walked off a little way and then suddenly turned round again.

'There's just one thing,' she said and her voice sounded quite normal now. 'Why on earth do you still carry those things around?' And she walked off.

Imogen gave a loud burst of laughter. 'Of course!' she cried. 'What idiots we all are not to have thought of it ourselves!' And she took off the cardboard box that was always on a string over her shoulder. She drew her arm back and threw the thing into the sea.

'Oh, Imogen, dare we?' said Julia and giggled nervously.

'What do you mean "dare we"? I've already done it!'

Julia got rid of hers as well, but not very confidently.

Imogen, on the other hand, was dancing about on the sand. Her unusual mood of a few minutes ago had completely changed.

'Come on, Meggy!' she cried. 'Yours next!'

Meggy hung on to it with both hands.

'Don't make me, don't make me!' she sobbed. 'I'm sure it isn't safe! We can't just throw them away!'

Imogen stopped dancing.

'Don't be silly, Meggy,' she said impatiently. 'Of course it's safe!'

'But what are they, what are they?' cried Helena. 'Why are you throwing them away?'

'They're just things that we got used to carrying all the time but now we don't need them,' said Imogen. 'Throw it away, Meggy!'

Julia suddenly tugged it off Meggy's shoulder and into the water it went.

Meggy screamed.

'Don't be so stupid,' said Imogen.

'I always thought they were lunch-boxes!' said Helena.

'Lunch-boxes!' said Imogen—and laughed and laughed. Perhaps she was overdoing it because, earlier on, she had been sad and subdued.

None of them would tell Helena what was in the boxes.

CHAPTER FIFTEEN

A Word Game

Henry declared that the day before the dress rehearsal was a day off for the whole company. This happened to be the day that Helena's other brother came to visit her—and Trevor spent the day with his parents again. Again, this was Robin's idea rather than Christine's. Helena went to meet James's train. She was actually quite looking forward to seeing him. The day felt like a real holiday.

James stepped off the train and walked, smiling, to where Helena was waiting at the barrier. She smiled back.

He was carrying a brown paper parcel under one arm which she glanced at curiously, but he didn't mention it until they were half-way to the beach. Then, 'Oh,' he said nonchalantly, 'Mum sent you this.'

He gave Helena the brown paper parcel. It had a label on it saying 'MISS HELENA RUTH WOODVINE'.

'What is it?' said Helena in surprise.

'Open it and see,' said James. They were passing by the pub right then so Helena sat down at the table outside it and started to pull at the Sellotape.

'I didn't mean open it in the street!' exclaimed James.

Helena tore away most of the brown paper and a flood of green material came out.

'She can't have made the dress already!' she said in astonishment.

'I think you'll find she has,' said James.

Almost reverently, Helena lifted her present out of the remaining paper and held it up.

It was a waisted dress that would fall to her calves when

she had it on. It had buttons all the way down the front, a V-shaped neckline with rounded lapels, and short sleeves. The material was green with small white diamonds all over it and the collar, the buttons, and the edges of the sleeves were white as well.

'It's beautiful,' said Helena. 'I never thought Mum would make it so quickly.'

'She bought the material the day after she saw you,' said James, 'and then sat up for two nights to get it finished for me to bring.'

For some reason, Helena couldn't look James in the eyes.

'So you see,' said James quietly. 'Mum isn't that bad after all. Is she?'

Helena went scarlet.

'I didn't think she was bad,' she muttered.

'You know what I mean,' said James.

Helena said nothing to that. Her eyes had suddenly filled with tears.

They diverted from their journey to the beach: Helena wanted to go back to the cottage first and change into the new dress.

James waited in the tiny living room while she was upstairs. He was taller than his twin brother and not as stocky. Too tall and thin for the room somehow. Helena could hear him moving about. He wasn't usually a restless person—maybe the room unnerved him. Maybe the strangeness of Serpenton had entered his blood and his nerves already.

There was only a small mirror in Helena's room, so when she had the dress on she had to bend down to see the top of it then stand on the bed to see the bottom of it. It was very frustrating not to see the whole effect all at once. Then she remembered there was a full-length mirror in the wardrobe door of Robin and Christine's room—so she went in there.

You get to Narnia through a wardrobe with a mirror, she thought absently as she made her way towards it.

But all other thoughts fled her head when she got the full view of herself in the dress in the mirror.

The garment fell in soft green folds over her body. It was good—she felt that it was.

After the first heart-stopping glow, a bit of hard, competitive pride hit her. My dress is better than Imogen's, she thought. And Julia's. And Meggy's. This one is the 'proper' material and a 'proper' length.

Then she felt oddly ashamed.

Usually she wouldn't. Not when it was the girls at home. They were always trying to out-trend each other.

The next feeling that came over her was the shyness she always had when she was wearing new clothes (not that that happened as often as she would have liked) and she had to face other people.

Would James like it? Was she fooling herself about how good it looked?

She went down the stairs much more slowly than usual, her heart beating hard. The door of the living room was open. James was standing on the threshold.

'You look lovely,' he said simply.

That was enough.

He opened the front door for her and she swooshed through it, feeling very 'actressy' in the flowing dress.

They took one more diversion before they got to the beach. Helena went to Mrs Fields's shop and bought a black and white postcard with a picture of Serpenton on it. On the back she wrote, 'Dear Mum. The dress is lovely. Thank you very much. With love from Helena'.

Mrs Fields sold stamps as well as all the other oddments. Helena posted the card in the box opposite the shop. As she was walking away from it, she realized that there were quite a lot of houses in Serpenton really. Even if there was only one person living in each one, there would still be enough people to make a fair-sized audience.

James kept looking to right and left, rather like their mother had.

'There's something about this place, isn't there?' he said.

'Yes,' said Helena shortly.

'There's a . . . there's an atmosphere here,' he said. 'I can't really explain it.'

'No,' said Helena.

'I'd like to find out about it. Its history, I mean.'

Helena stared at him fearfully. She didn't want him to do any delving. He might find out things about the theatre company that she didn't want to know.

'*The Roses of Eyam*,' he said unexpectedly. 'Do you remember that play? It was about the plague.'

'Of course I remember it.' As if there would be a play that he knew and she didn't!

'That was only a small village but it had a big, historical moment. Maybe this place did too. You never know.'

His words fell into Helena's head as clearly as stones thrown in the sea. And the ripples they sent out made her dizzy.

'Let's walk on the beach,' she said faintly, hoping to shut him up.

The beach today was more towards the yellow than the grey. A mellowish mood. For now anyway. Sometimes, the scattered stones and bits of shell looked jagged and sharp enough to tear a bare foot to pieces. Today they were rounded and blunted. Helena and her brother both took their boots and socks off. They walked along the sand, the boots hanging down from their hands by the laces. The white foam gently dashed on the pebbles a bit further off; the seagulls were sending out muted cries. Neither Helena nor

James spoke for a few minutes—so the atmosphere swept over and round them. It was like going 'under' with ether gas.

Helena could have stayed in that state of absorption all day. But James wasn't really an outdoor sort of person: he broke the spell.

'Let's sit down now,' he said, and then twirled round as if looking for something.

'Is there a deck-chair attendant here?' he said.

Helena took a long time to come back from the 'ether gas' feeling.

'What?' she said vaguely. 'Deck-chairs?'

'I thought there were always deck-chairs at the seaside.'

'Not this seaside.'

'Oh. Well, these rocks will have to do then.'

He took his jacket off and was about to sit on it when he realized that Helena didn't have one and, because she was wearing a brand new dress, he gave her his, first taking a paperback book from his inside pocket. He settled down to read with a sigh of contentment.

Helena shifted about on his jacket and sat on a pocket with something hard in it.

'What's this?' she said and drew it out. It was a hard-backed notebook almost used up. She flicked through it and had glimpses of crosswords and puzzles and linked-up sentences, patterned with arrows. If looking at a globe meant looking at the whole world, then looking at this book could mean looking at the whole of James's personality. Towards the end of the book there were pairs of words going down the page joined by lines.

'What's this one?' asked Helena. Some of the words in the lists were rather intriguing.

'It's a word game,' said James. 'Someone showed it me last week.'

Helena peered at some more of the words.

'Let's have a go then.'

James was delighted. He put the paperback down and suddenly wielded an expensive-looking pen as if from nowhere.

'Pass me the book, please, Helena,' he said, 'and give me twelve words.'

For some reason, Helena thought fleetingly of a jury and twelve people on it . . .

'Twelve words,' she murmured. 'What sort of words?'

'Any sort. Nice words. Words you like.'

'Stage. Curtain . . . Er . . . trapdoor.'

James looked at her narrowly.

'All right then,' he said and wrote them down.

'Trapdoor. Er . . . Costume. Script. How many's that?'

'Five.'

'Prop.'

'What?'

'Prop. You know, as in stage prop.'

'That's short for property.'

'Is it? Well, property, then.'

'Six more.'

'Scenery. Er . . . er . . . ticket.'

'Helena,' said James.

'Yes?'

'They don't all have to follow the same theme, you know.'

'Programme. Er . . . Audience. How many more?'

'Two.'

'Footlight. Spotlight.'

James didn't say anything for a few seconds.

'What's the matter?' said Helena.

'Has it been really terrible looking after that Melling kid?'

'Why do you ask that?'

'Well, all those theatrical words. You're still wishing you

were doing the local play at home, aren't you? Instead of being here and looking after Trevor, I mean.'

'No,' said Helena quite truthfully. 'I'm not wishing that at all.'

'Are you sure?'

'Yes.'

He didn't look very convinced but he shrugged his shoulders and carried on with the game.

'Now,' he said. 'You have to connect the words up. You do it in pairs going down the list. Your first two words are "stage" and "curtain". Think of a word—any word—that would connect the two. And it doesn't have to be theatrical, Lenna.'

But Helena obstinately said, 'Wings. You know, as in "waiting in the wings". The wings are at the sides and you stand there while you're waiting to go on stage and . . .'

'Thank you, but I know what they are, Helena.' And he wrote down 'wings' with a slight frown. 'Next is "trapdoor" and "costume".'

'Ghost. You know, someone wearing a ghost's costume and disappearing down a trapdoor.'

' "Script" and "property".'

Helena thought for a while and then said 'Pen.'

'I don't see how . . . '

'You write the script with a pen and you could have a pen for a prop, couldn't you?'

'Hmm,' said James. 'That one's a bit shaky.'

'What's the next one?'

'I haven't decided whether to accept "pen" yet.'

'You're so pompous!'

'No, I'm not!'

'Yes you are!'

'All right, all right, I'll accept "Pen",' said James hastily. Then he said ' "Scenery" and "ticket".'

'Railway. You wanted one that wasn't theatrical. Railway.'

'Well done. "Programme" and "audience".'

'Er . . . Enlighten.'

'My God, that's a good one!'

'Well, don't sound so surprised!'

'Sorry. "Footlight" and "spotlight".'

'Dazzle.'

'Right, that's another list now. A shorter one. You do the same with that. "Wings" and "ghost".'

'I suppose the obvious one is angel but I don't want angel,' said Helena. 'I know, Devil. That's a much better word.'

'Now is the Devil, strictly speaking, a ghost?' said James in his most 'intellectual' voice.

'Oh, just put it down!' said Helena impatiently.

He looked a bit ruffled, but wrote it down. ' "Pen" and "railway".'

'Clerk. You know, when you buy your ticket at the office, there's a man who . . . '

'Thank you, Helena, but you don't need to explain everything. I'm not that stupid. "Enlighten" and "dazzle".'

'What's that word for when you have a blinding flash of something or other?'

'You what?'

'A blinding flash of something or other.'

'Could you mean a revelation?' he asked, verging on the pompous again.

'Yes I could,' said Helena stonily—with a lot more meaning to that adverb than there used to be.

A pause.

Then:

'Now you see we've made an even shorter list and we do it again. There's only three words this time so

126

you have to repeat the middle one. Now, "Devil" and "clerk".'

'Magician,' said Helena. 'They have dealings with the Devil sometimes and they write—you know, runes and things so they can be sort of clerks as well.'

James looked at her but she stared obstinately back—so he just shrugged and wrote down 'Magician'.

' "Clerk" and "Revelation",' he said next.

'I can't do that one!'

'Yes, you can. Think!'

'Oh, I don't know. Ether. No. Yes, though. Ether.'

'What? That must be the most obscure yet!'

' Ether,' said Helena, thinking quickly. 'A mere clerk could have a revelation under the effects of ether gas.'

'I don't believe this,' said James faintly.

'Just write it down,' she said yet again.

Another pause while he did it slowly.

'This is the last bit now,' he said, 'and it will make your final word. "Magician" and "Ether".'

'Making magic and putting you under,' murmured Helena dreamily. 'Playwrights do that, don't they? Playwright.'

And then she found herself thinking about Miss Smith. How strange: out of all the people she could have come up with, her final word was the occupation of the person she liked the least.

'Oh, Lenna, you'd have chosen that whatever the last two words were!' said James with no knowledge of Miss Smith's existence at all.

'No, I wouldn't.'

'Are you sure you're not still thinking about the Drama Society at home?'

'Quite sure.'

The completed game looked like this:

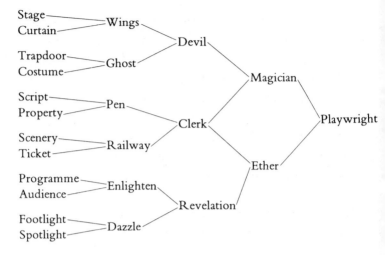

Miss Smith's play about the sea serpent was very good, there was no doubt about that. In her capacity as playwright, whether professional or not, Helena had a lot of respect for her. It was as a person she found her so hard to relate to. She went quiet and thought about it.

'Made you think, hasn't it?' said James.

'What?'

'The word-game. It does that to people. They're often surprised by what they come up with—things they wouldn't expect to. And sometimes they're even frightened.'

Involuntarily, Helena shivered.

The sound of people approaching made them both look up, and they saw Imogen, Julia, and Meggy walking along the edge of the sea.

'Hello!' shouted Helena.

'Good afternoon!' James called to them pleasantly.

Well, he's behaving normally with them anyway, thought Helena with relief. He wasn't acting like Christopher had.

But the three girls had started violently. They stopped

dead and stared at him. He didn't notice them doing that because his head was down over the word-game again. But Helena noticed.

'What's the matter?' she called.

They were speaking together in whispers.

'It's all right!' shouted Helena. 'This is my other brother. He won't be rude to you like Christopher was.'

'Was Chris rude to them?' said James in surprise.

'Yes, it was quite strange really,' said Helena. 'He just completely ignored them as if he didn't see them.'

She was very anxious to believe it was just rudeness on Christopher's part—not something more mysterious.

'Are they friends of yours?' asked James.

'Yes, of course they are. Come over here!' she shouted to them.

They hesitated, conferred for a little longer and then slowly walked towards them, Imogen in front and the other two behind, still whispering. They all looked strangely excited. Helena heard the last part of what Julia and Meggy were saying, though they probably hadn't intended her to.

'There must be some reason!' said Julia. 'Perhaps we'll be all right—you know, after the play. Perhaps after all, we won't just . . . you know . . . '

'It's probably because he's sensitive,' said Meggy dreamily. 'He looks sensitive, doesn't he?'

'He really isn't as good looking as her other brother, you know, Meggy,' said Julia earnestly.

He's a lot nicer though, thought Helena. And it's a matter of opinion anyway.

She introduced them all to her brother and he asked Meggy if her name was short for Margaret.

'No,' she said shyly. 'It's Megan.'

'That's a lovely name,' said James and she went bright red.

They talked about this and that. Everyone was careful not

to mention the theatre company because then James would know Helena wasn't looking after Trevor in quite the way that was intended. Even Julia didn't put her foot in it. Not at that point anyway. They said they liked Helena's dress but she got the impression it was more out of politeness than anything else.

'Don't you like your shorts any more, Helena?' said Meggy.

'I'm sick of wearing dresses like this myself,' said Julia.

No one said anything to that.

Then Julia spoke again.

'You'll miss her, won't you?' she said curiously to James.

'Miss who?' said James and Helena both together.

Time thumped.

'Oh, no one,' said Julia lamely.

Helena could feel the inexplicable panic mounting again. James saved it from getting worse.

'I've just taught Helena a word-game,' he said. 'Shall I teach it to you three as well?'

Then his face fell.

'No more pages left,' he said, opening his notebook at the back.

'You can write on the sand,' said Imogen. 'It's nice and firm. All you've got to do is find a sharp stick.'

'Will that work?' said James doubtfully.

'Of course it will!' said Helena. She and Julia and Imogen started hunting among the seaweed and shells for a sharp stick. Meggy stayed where she was and gazed at James. He smiled at her—and her eyes shot to the ground at once. She went bright red again.

They found a stick and James held it like a pen in his hand. Imogen had first go and he wrote her words carefully in the sand. She rattled off twelve clever words in fast succession; then six, then three, then two—then her final word was 'capability'.

Julia was next, giggling all the way through. Her last word was 'handsome'.

'Now your turn, Meggy,' said James kindly.

Meggy stared at him.

'Oh come on, Meggy!' said Imogen impatiently. 'You can think of twelve words surely!'

Meggy's lip started to tremble.

'I can't,' she said.

'Oh, don't be stupid. Of course you can.'

'I can't! I'm no good at that sort of thing.'

'Oh, Meggy, you're so wet!' said Imogen.

'She doesn't have to play if she doesn't want to,' said James uncomfortably.

'She never wants to do anything,' said Julia. 'She's boring.'

'Gas mask!' Meggy suddenly screamed at the top of her voice. 'That's my first word. Gas mask!'

Helena jumped violently and stared at Meggy in amazement.

'Now, Meggy,' said Imogen in a dangerous voice. 'That's an odd word to choose now, isn't it? Whatever made you think of that, Meggy?'

'You know why!' cried Meggy.

'And anyway you can't have it,' said Julia, 'because it's two words, not one.'

'Think of another word, Meggy,' said Imogen—and the way she said it sent shivers down Helena's spine.

'Ration book!' Meggy screamed.

'That's two words again, Meggy,' said Imogen. 'You can't have them—' And she grabbed hold of Meggy's wrist. 'Pull yourself together,' she said evenly.

But Meggy was struggling like a terrified child.

'Wireless!' she cried. 'Aeroplane! Bomb!'

Imogen tightened her grip on Meggy's wrist and clapped her other hand over her mouth. Meggy didn't say any more but the tears were streaming down her face and her body shook with sobs.

'I . . . er . . . I think it's time we forgot the word-game,' said James. He looked at Helena. They were both pale and shocked. Julia was gnawing at her lip.

'Let go of Meggy, please, Imogen,' said James.

Imogen looked at him, then took her hand away from Meggy's mouth. Meggy didn't utter a sound. Imogen released her wrist, and Meggy sank in a heap on the rocks. James sat down as well. So did Helena. Their legs were shaking.

'I think we should go now,' said Imogen quietly. 'Meggy isn't very well. Come on, Julia.' She and Julia helped Meggy to her feet and led her away.

The weather had changed. The sky was surly now and the seagulls' cries more persistent and heart-lurching than they had been earlier.

CHAPTER SIXTEEN

The Dress Rehearsal

On the day of the dress rehearsal, which was to be in the evening, Helena nearly had a heart attack in the late afternoon.

This was caused by Christine suddenly announcing that she and Robin would be going out that evening with their new friends—so Helena would be left with Trevor. They hadn't been out in the evening for a few days—just done their socializing during the day—so Helena had been lulled into a false sense of security. She had thought she was safe for both the evenings of the dress rehearsal and the performance. But now she was forced into wondering whether Monica would deal with Trevor in the evening. Suppose she said no? Suppose she considered the evenings her own?

'But I'm going out myself!' Helena blurted out at the tea table. 'I'm meeting some . . . some friends!'

What Christine would have said to this, she was never to know, because Trevor, after eyeing Helena in a knowing kind of way, suddenly clutched his little guts and fell off his chair.

'Mummy, Mummy!' he cried.

'What, what?' Christine replied in horror while Robin scooped him up.

'It hurts, it hurts! You can't leave me, you can't leave me!'

As he was being borne upstairs, he winked unmistakably at Helena over his father's shoulder.

An hour later, as she was getting ready to go out, she felt rather solemn. She realized she was filled with awe over how a seven-year-old child had helped her—and the same seven-year-old she had detested at the start of the summer.

The door to the 'costume room' was opened at half-past six. Everyone stood and looked silently into it—and then they all crowded in at once. There was a great feeling of excitement.

'Good God, look at these!' said Solomon, holding out a pair of trousers and a shirt. Everyone burst out laughing.

'Will you enjoy getting back into civvies?' somebody asked him.

'What are "civvies"?' Helena whispered to Imogen.

'What he's got in his hand,' said Imogen. 'Civilian clothing.'

Helena still looked puzzled so she added, 'Your ordinary clothes. What you wear when you're not in uniform. Or costume, in our case.'

And Helena suddenly realized how odd it was that Solomon had been dressed like a pieman the whole time she had known him—and he wasn't a pieman in real life! He was a pieman only in the play.

'So he's been wearing his costume the whole time then!' she said. 'Why does he do that?'

'These are yours, Helena,' said Imogen without answering her. She pointed to a set of clothes hanging neatly on a hook with a label pinned on them saying 'Stoney Vale'. They were rough, hand-made things; a white shirt with criss-cross boot lacing up the front instead of buttons, a skirt and waistcoat which looked as if they had been made out of old curtains and a pair of breeches as well.

'Do I wear the skirt or the breeches?' asked Helena.

'Both,' said Imogen. 'The skirt's for the earlier scenes when you don't do gymnastics and the breeches for the scenes when you do.'

'So that I don't show my knickers,' said Helena, looking sideways at Miss Smith. Miss Smith looked appalled. Helena and Julia hung on to each other and laughed.

'Oh, Imogen,' said someone when Imogen was in her costume. 'Don't forget Vivien wouldn't be wearing stockings.' (Vivien was the name of the character Imogen played.)

'Oh, of course,' said Imogen—but she didn't take her stockings off in the usual way. She passed two finger tips across her tongue and started rubbing at the seams down the back of her legs. To Helena's amazement, the seams started disappearing!

'They're not real ones!' she cried. Everyone turned and stared at her. 'You've just put seams down your legs with a pen!'

Imogen laughed uproariously. 'Eyebrow pencil to be exact!' she said. 'And don't you think my legs are a convincing colour?' She held out a brown leg which, up till then, Helena had believed was brown because she was wearing stockings (or tights, as she had thought).

'Gravy browning,' said Imogen.

'It's a real saving on stockings,' somebody else assured Helena.

Helena and most of her friends at home wore tights rather than stockings.

Everyone was laughing and joking and having a good time—except for Meggy. Helena had said nothing to her about what had happened the day before and Imogen and Julia were steering clear of her altogether. She looked pale and strained and, every so often, would glance fearfully around the hall as if she was scared it would all fall down! The sight of her sobered Helena after a while.

The soberness started spreading to other people too. The

dress rehearsal was due to begin at half-past seven—and, by quarter past, there was no smiling or laughing left in the whole place. Now, they were a silent, twitching band of players waiting to make their first entrances. Even though she was quite nervous herself, Helena couldn't really understand the extent of their twitchiness. After all, it was only the dress rehearsal, not the public performance. Nobody would be watching them! But they were acting as if they were about to be executed.

The dress rehearsal began. Everyone was worked up to fever pitch by now. Henry, sitting in his director's chair at the back of the hall, was no more relaxed than anyone else. He clenched his fists and gritted his teeth all the way through the livelier scenes—and even in the quiet scenes he drummed his fingers on the edge of his chair.

There wasn't much 'set' to speak of—just props really. They brought on a lamp-post for the scenes in the village square, and for the beach scenes, they threw some floppy pieces of artificial seaweed around. These were made of material lightly stuffed with old stockings (tights?). They were like limp, wiggly draught excluders, all in purple and green. No one had tried to create an artificial sea serpent, either by making a stuffed one or by dressing up and acting as one. As Henry said, it would have been too silly. Most of the dealings with the serpent were 'reported' by other characters and not actually seen by the audience. In the last scene, when Stoney Vale was believed to have gone off to the serpent forever, all the crowd gathered together among the stuffed seaweed and looked off-stage. This was where the sea was supposed to be.

At the end of the dress rehearsal, a dead silence fell on the whole company. Helena was expecting Henry to clap, because he was all the audience there was—but he didn't. He just got up and said, 'That was good. Now let's pack everything away.' Like sleep-walkers, they all obeyed. Helena was getting tenser and tenser. She felt as if she almost couldn't bear it.

'Shall I leave my pieman costume on again?' asked Solomon.

'No, Solly,' said Henry. 'Put your ordinary clothes on this time.'

'It'll feel very odd after all this time,' said Solly. 'I always did prefer my costume to my civvies.'

Dumbly, they all changed into their own clothes and hung the costumes back on the hooks. Imogen took an eyebrow pencil out of her pocket and drew seams up the back of her legs again. Julia brushed her hair and put clips in it. Meggy didn't do anything but stood there and looked terrified.

Suddenly, Helena could stand no more.

'I'm going out for a few minutes,' she said, her voice cracking with strain. 'I'm going to walk to those trees where it's cool.'

Meggy gave a loud scream and Julia grabbed Helena's arm.

'No, no, you mustn't!' she cried. 'Do you want to get left all on your own like Mon—'

'Be quiet, Julia,' said Imogen. 'And please stay here, Helena.'

'But you're all giving me the creeps!' cried Helena. 'Why are you being like this? There's something so strange about you all—I notice things all the time! I—' but she stopped there, taking control again, knowing she had to, remembering what Monica had said.

And nobody answered her. She saw Henry look at his watch and then at Solomon. Solomon looked at his watch too. He nodded at Henry, biting his lip. Meggy dashed underneath a table and curled up like a hamster with her head down. Helena might have laughed at that if she hadn't been feeling so tense and awful. Everyone was looking up at the ceiling now. Five heavy minutes went by.

'Dad,' said Imogen—and everyone jumped. They stared at her with faces as white as paper. 'Dad,' she said again, 'it's going to be all right this time, isn't it?'

All eyes turned on Henry. He looked at his watch again and a smile crept slowly over his face.

'Yes, Imogen,' he said quietly. 'This time the people of Serpenton are going to get their play.'

It was a ridiculously overdramatic thing to say but it didn't make Helena want to laugh. She looked around her, startled, because everyone else was cheering! Meggy came out from under the table. She was still shaking slightly but there was a dawn of a smile on her face.

'You can go out to the trees now if you want to, Helena!' cried Julia. 'It's all right now.'

But Helena didn't want to any more. She suddenly felt as joyful as anyone else—although the last few minutes had been such a strain.

Whatever had come over them all?

CHAPTER SEVENTEEN

A Letter

It was quite early the next morning, and Helena should either have been asleep or thinking only about the play that night. But she was doing neither.

She was tearing through the streets of Serpenton, not seeming to notice that they twisted like a maze. The tears were streaming down her face and she was clutching a letter in her hand.

The letter had arrived for her that morning and it was from her brother, James. She had only read it once and now she was dashing straight to Monica's house.

When she got there—wild-eyed and gasping for breath—Monica was already standing at the front door.

'How did you know I was coming?' Helena almost screamed.

'I just knew,' said Monica sadly and drew her inside. 'Who's the letter from?' she asked, looking at the crumpled square of white in Helena's hand.

'James. My brother,' said Helena and gave it to her, her hand shaking. Then she sat down.

Monica sat in the opposite chair and read the letter.

This was it:

'Dear Helena,

I told you I'd find out about the history of Serpenton. I didn't think it would be so soon though. Do you remember Greg—who I was at school with? His sister knows Sophie Miller who's the one the Mellings rent the cottage from. Apparently, during the Second World War, the villagers in Serpenton wanted to put a play on as a way of getting everyone involved in something and cheering them all up. So they put a theatre company together and they were going to do it on top of that hill behind the village because there used to be a hall there. Odd, wasn't it? But the play was never performed. On the night of the dress rehearsal, a stray bomb landed on the village hall and they were all killed—except one. Apparently there was a teenage girl who said she was too hot and went out to stand under some trees a little way off from the hall—so she was saved. And Sophie Miller said she's still living there in the village! Wouldn't it be exciting to . . .'

Monica didn't read any more but let the paper fall from her hand to the floor. Helena heard it rustle and slide and she looked up. She gazed at Monica through a fog. Her contact lenses had clouded over. Monica smiled anxiously and they leaned forward and embraced each other.

'Monica!' sobbed Helena.

'I know,' said Monica. 'You're terrified, aren't you? Terrified and upset.'

'You were Stoney Vale first. It was you!'

'Specially chosen,' said Monica. 'For my . . . ' she faltered.

'Strange hypnotic powers,' Helena filled in for her. 'Stoney Vale is a strange part so they chose someone . . . er . . . '

This time, Monica finished the sentence: 'Strange to play it,' she said, without flinching. Maybe she was proud of being strange.

There was a pause.

'Does that mean I'm strange too?' Helena asked, not knowing whether she wanted to hear a reply or not.

Monica just smiled.

'It isn't just that!' said Helena rather desperately.

'No, of course it isn't,' said Monica, which pacified her slightly. 'There's something about the part—it has glamour to it.'

'It's magical,' said Helena.

They looked at each other and agreed.

'Imogen was furious at first that she didn't get it,' said Monica—and she sounded like a victorious fourteen-year-old, but only for a moment. 'But then we all got so caught up with . . . you know . . . '

'Yes,' murmured Helena. ' "The smell of the greasepaint, the roar of the crowds . . . " '

Her quoting 'the roar of the crowds' brought them both back down to earth. After all, Monica had missed out on that in her time . . .

'It was such a fluke, you know, what happened,' said Monica. 'It was just like that letter says. I was too hot after the dress rehearsal so I wandered away to cool off. Quite a way from the hall—right over to where that furthest clump of trees is. And then . . . well, for a long time afterwards, I wished I'd gone with them all. I thought it was better than being left on my own. But we all knew they'd come back. We all knew in the village: the play still had to be done and to be seen. Serpenton could only half exist until it was played out.'

'But why?' said Helena. 'Why did it pull at you all so strongly?'

'Because of the spirit it was put together in!' said Monica. 'It was something that involved the whole village in one way or another. People had never got on with each other better. It was war time—and it was something to focus on to get us through it! The most surprising things came to light too. Who would have thought Claire Smith could write like that for one thing?'

'I would never have thought it,' mumbled Helena.

'She had files and files of things all stashed away that nobody knew about and she never thought she would do anything with. But she only needed the chance—like anyone does—and it came then. The production couldn't just come to nothing! The spirit and energy of it all were too strong.'

Helena could relate to that all right. She felt dizzy with all the things that were suddenly falling into place in her head. The things she thought were lunch-boxes were gas masks! Everyone was supposed to carry them all the time during the war. Her father had told her that. The twenty-eight-year-old lover in the play was played by a forty-five-year-old man because all the young men at the time were away at war. They had all stared at her as she ate the banana because bananas weren't delivered to England in the war. Stockings were in short supply as well—so Imogen made her legs brown with gravy-browning and put seams up the back with an eyebrow pencil. Solomon wore his pieman costume all the time now because he hadn't yet changed back into civvies when the bomb fell. Miss Smith tried to pay for her handkerchief with old-fashioned pennies and was stopped by Imogen who realized the currency would be different. And on and on and on . . .

She felt a great pang when she thought about Imogen, Julia, and Meggy—never to grow older and meet anyone. 'Meeting someone' seemed to be one of the bigger quests—all the books and films told you that. It wasn't surprising those three had been so interested in Christopher, who presumably just simply hadn't seen them. And Trevor wouldn't have seen any of them either. Only Helena had been granted 'special licence' because she was the next Stoney Vale. But wait a minute—there was James. James had seen them. James had actually seen them!

'Monica,' said Helena. 'Why did James see Imogen and Julia and Meggy? My brother, I mean. Why did he see them? He wasn't anything to do with the play. No wonder they were so startled when he spoke to them!'

'Yes, that was bizarre,' said Monica. 'I heard about it. It raised the most tremendous hope in those three girls, you know. They think maybe their time is going to stretch beyond the performance of the play after all but . . . well, who knows? Maybe he's got something he has to do—like you have—which is why he was able to see things other people couldn't. And anyway, he's your favourite, isn't he? In your family, I mean.'

'He's the one who likes me the best,' said Helena rather stubbornly.

'Really?' said Monica. 'More than your mother? I don't think so.'

This was a new idea to Helena. Even though she was wearing the green dress her mother had made. She stared speechlessly at Monica, her face still raw from the shocks she had had.

Monica Blaze spoke again:

'Of course, I kept hoping they would all come back sooner—so I could still play Stoney Vale. But they didn't. And now I'm too old. They waited fifty years. For some reason. And you're my replacement.'

Helena was overcome with horror.

'Do you mean I've still got to do it?' she cried. 'I've still got to do it even now I know they're all . . . they're all ghosts?'

Monica gripped Helena's arm.

'Of course you must do it,' she said—and now her voice was stern. 'Do you think I've given up any hope of doing it myself and then waited for fifty years only for you to let us all down at the end? You've been chosen! Whether you like it or not, you've got to do it now!'

'But what happens afterwards?' Helena whispered. 'When it's all over? Will they all just . . . disappear? And what will I do?'

Monica relented.

'It will be all right,' she said, if somewhat awkwardly. 'I'm sure it will be all right.'

Helena wished she had said 'I know' instead of 'I'm sure'.

But she knew she would go through with it. She couldn't help it.

CHAPTER EIGHTEEN

The Performance

As Helena arrived back at the cottage and made her way upstairs, she heard a muffled call from Trevor's room.

She went in at once.

He was sitting up in bed in his bright blue pyjamas with the yellow borders. He grinned at her. There was a jug of water by his bed, carefully covered, and his glass with the robots on.

'Are you better, Trevor?' asked Helena, hoping to God he wasn't because she needed Robin and Christine to stay in again that evening.

Trevor gazed at her with wide, innocent eyes.

'Do you want me to be better, Helena?' he asked.

She grinned.

'No, Trevor, I don't,' she said in equally innocent tones. 'Not until tomorrow.'

Trevor obliged at once.

'Oh, it hurts, it still hurts,' he cried and rolled around in the bed.

'Stop a minute,' said Helena. 'I want to hug you.'

As Helena arrived at the entrance to the village hall that evening, she saw Imogen sitting in there with a pile of programmes. Miss Smith was standing by her, waiting, her leather case in her hand. Neither of them had seen Helena, so she stood back a moment and watched them. Imogen was altering something in each one of the programmes with a pen. When she had finished, she gave them to Miss Smith and said, 'Hand them out to everyone but, whatever you do, don't give one to Monica.'

Miss Smith nodded and moved off to the other end of the hall. Then Imogen looked up and saw Helena.

'Good God, Helena,' she cried in alarm, 'what's the matter with you? You look as if you've . . . '

'Seen a ghost?' Helena finished for her.

There was a deadly silence for a moment.

'So how do you feel?' asked Imogen carefully.

Helena was very relieved it was Imogen she was dealing with, not Meggy.

'Scared,' she replied.

But then something dawned on her:

'But I would be anyway,' she said. 'I'm in a play tonight! There's an audience coming!'

Imogen laughed in a measured sort of way. Then she said, 'Wait there a moment.'

Helena watched her move to the other end of the hall where a few of the others were gathered, talking. She went up to her father and said something to him. He spun round at once to look at Helena but Imogen restrained him—and he felt in his jacket pocket and brought something out which he gave to her. Helena saw it gleam as it changed hands—it was a hard, silver object. Imogen carried it over to her and revealed it for a small flask with a screw top.

'Have some of this,' said Imogen.

'What is it?'

'It's a spice drink. My mum used to make it—it's her recipe. She said it's the best thing for nerves: it's got lots of ginger in it—and cloves and cinnamon and hot fruit juices. Get it down you. It might help.'

Helena took a large swig and gasped.

'More,' said Imogen softly. 'Have more.'

Helena had more—not caring for the taste, but gradually succumbing to the stinging, ginger glow that came over her.

'Oh, that's better,' she said.

Imogen took hold of her hand.

'What do I feel like?' she asked. 'Do I feel cold and vaporous?'

'Vaporous,' said Helena dreamily. 'What a lovely word . . . '

'But is that what I feel like?'

'No.'

'What do I feel like?'

'Warm skin.'

'Like yours.'

'But—'

'Stoney Vale,' said Imogen. 'Don't you want to be Stoney Vale tonight?'

'Yes,' said Helena. 'I do.'

'Stage nerves,' said Imogen. 'That's all you feel. Stage nerves.'

The two of them moved to the dressing room to get ready —the living and the returned, ready to deal with the unfinished business.

From half-past six to a quarter-past seven, a stream of people climbed the High Hat. The door of the village hall was wedged open and Henry and Miss Smith were standing on either side of it to greet the people as they arrived. Miss Smith was handing out the programmes. She wasn't doing it very well because her hand was shaking. Every so often, someone would say, 'Claire Smith, how lovely to see you again! What a relief this must be to you!'

'Yes,' she would reply faintly, looking at the speakers as if she didn't recognize them.

Henry, on the other hand, was showing no signs of agitation at all. He smiled confidently at everyone and his handshake was firm. A lot of the audience were elderly people—as lively and bright-eyed as children, taking their seats quickly. Peering at them round the edge of the costume room door, Helena was very touched. She saw Mrs Fields quite near the front sitting next to the guard from the station.

There were two minutes to go and the hall was completely full except for three chairs at the back. Then there was one minute to go and Miss Smith sat down on one of them, carefully putting the remaining programmes in her leather case. Henry stayed waiting by the door. Half a minute to go and the last member of the audience appeared, rather uncertainly, at the door. Henry stepped forward and embraced her. Both of them had tears in their eyes. He led her to a chair.

'Monica Blaze has come,' hissed Julia, who had taken over from Helena at the door of the costume room. 'That'll be it now!'

The people in the opening scene got ready to step on the platform. The most almighty rush of nerves came sweeping over Helena—genuine stage nerves now, not suggested ones to cover up something else.

Henry turned the lights off at the back of the hall. There was a moment of deep silence when everyone sat in the darkness; then he turned them on again and the play began.

The opening scene had everyone in it except Helena, Imogen, Julia, Meggy and a woman called Dorothy, who played Stoney's aunt.

Helena sat in the costume room, sweating and shaking.

'Whatever's the matter?' whispered Julia.

'I . . . I'm so nervous!' wheezed Helena. She could hardly get the words out.

'I'm not,' said Julia.

Helena stared at her in amazement.

'But you were for the dress rehearsal yesterday!'

'That was different.'

'Why was it different?'

'Because . . . ' and then Julia saw Imogen's eyes on her and lamely said, 'Because it just was.'

I know why, Helena thought to herself. It was because yesterday was the dress rehearsal and that was the day you all got killed before . . .

But she thought of it in a detached way—as if nothing could affect her now, except fear of the immediate.

A sudden burst of clapping indicated the end of the first scene. The players came off the platform, sweating and grinning. Imogen, Julia, and Meggy shot on for the second scene.

'It's going brilliantly!' said the forty-five-year-old man who played the twenty-eight-year-old lover.

'Like a dream,' said Solly the pieman and his eyes glistened.

The second scene with the three girls was quite short—and then the third scene had just two people in it: Stoney Vale and her aunt, Miss Emma Vale. Helena's legs were shaking so much, she could hardly get on the platform. Her first line, which was quite a funny one, came out of her mouth in a high-pitched squeak—or so it seemed to her. To her sheer amazement, the audience laughed just the same. She began to calm down. Before the scene was half over, she was more than calmed down—she was positively enjoying herself.

The play went by on wings. After Helena's first hand-walking scene, the audience cheered. When the young couple were talking on the beach, the forty-five-year-old man was so lyrical that Helena really believed he was only twenty-eight. He gazed into his lover's eyes and you wouldn't believe he couldn't see a thing. They wouldn't let him wear his glasses for the part and Helena, of course, now knew why he had never seen contact lenses before.

Meggy forgot one of her lines at one point but Imogen smoothly sandwiched it between two of hers, so nobody knew. When it came to the scene where Stoney gives her precious stones and shells away, Henry had told Helena to go among the audience and give some to them too. Helena had been dreading this because she thought it would be terribly embarrassing. But it wasn't! The people took them quite seriously. Mrs Fields even said, 'Thank you, Stoney.'

Everyone was on stage for the last scene, looking out to the 'sea'. Stoney had already disappeared. That was the last time they would ever see her. Now there were only three more lines to go: Imogen, as Vivien, had the first one; Dorothy, playing Stoney's Aunt Emma, had the second— and Solomon, as the pieman, said the last. They all froze where they stood and Henry turned the lights off again.

Complete darkness, complete silence.

Then he turned them on and such a storm of clapping blew up it was nearly deafening. Helena had stepped back on the stage while it was dark. The players all joined hands and bowed. The clapping got louder and louder. People started rising to their feet and cheering. Solomon and Dorothy detached themselves from the stage and went to the back of the hall. Solly took Miss Smith's arm and Dorothy took Henry's. They led them to the platform and the author and the director had a bow of their own.

The play was over.

After that, Helena was in a complete whirl of joy—the way she usually was when a performance had been a success. Nothing else seemed to be registering for her any more. The players and the villagers were mingling and people were saying nice things to her on every side. She didn't notice whether Monica was there for that bit or not—but she did notice when Imogen was flashing her father's silver flask at her again.

'Yes please,' she said at once. Down her throat went the tawny liquid. She winced at the taste and then relaxed as the glow started—stronger now than it was before.

'So you're all ghosts!' she cried at one point. 'So what? You're my friends!'

'Stay a bit longer, Helena,' said Imogen. 'Don't go home yet.'

'Oh no, I don't want to!'

In a blur, Helena heard Solly say something.

'What are you playing at, Imogen?'

'She might prefer it with us!' said Imogen defensively. 'She loves being Stoney Vale! It pulls at her like it did Monica. And look at the sad life Monica's had—all on her own for all those years, without us.'

'She had the other people in the village!'

'She'd rather have been with us. Helena might too. She doesn't get on with her mother—she told us. She might not want to go back home to her!'

Helena looked around the room, her head spinning. She noticed there was a large crack in the wall which would have disturbed her more than it did if she hadn't been euphoric.

Everyone had changed into their 'civvies' now. The costumes were hanging in the changing room, neatly on hangers.

'We don't need to bother now, do we?' Julia had said, all prepared to just sling her costume on the floor.

But her father had said, 'Yes, we do. Otherwise, it'll feel like unfinished business again.'

'But . . . ' her voice trailed off and she hung her costume up.

The only people left in the hall now were the players. All the villagers had gone.

Everything was terribly neat and tidy—almost uncannily so. Someone had even swept the place and then conscientiously put the broom back in its cupboard in the Ladies' toilet. There were no spiders' webs anywhere— Helena had made a point of looking although her vision was slightly hazy. The only disturbing, disrupting thing was the crack in the wall—the same wall that had the poster stuck on it saying 'Careless Talk Costs Lives'.

'Has that crack always been there?' asked Helena, surprised at the difficulty she had getting the words out. 'I've never noticed it before.'

'Helena,' said someone rather timidly. 'Shouldn't you be going home now?'

She turned round and saw Meggy. She felt confused.

'I don't know,' she said. 'Should I?'

There was a sudden great thump and swish. Part of the ceiling had fallen down near the door. Plaster and rubble smoked with dust on the floor.

Meggy had shrieked loudly and then stood staring at someone who had arrived at the open door.

'You,' she said simply.

'Yes, me,' said Monica.

They had left the door wedged open because the evening was warm. There was a glimpse of green and a stillness beyond.

Most of the theatre company seemed to be frozen now, staring at the door. Imogen was the only one still shifting. She was moving her father's silver flask from one hand to the other.

Monica cleared her throat.

'I've come for Helena,' she said. 'It's time she was leaving here now.'

'But she's not sure she wants to,' said Imogen at once.

There was a loud crack and Helena turned her head to see that the window had a spiders' web pattern that hadn't been there before.

'The place is falling in,' said Monica evenly. 'Its work is done and now it will collapse. Helena needs to leave here. Now.'

She said the 'now' like a whip cracking.

An idea was slowly forming in Helena's head.

'But it's a ghost hall,' she said drowsily. 'If it falls down, it can't hurt me.'

'I wouldn't be so sure of that,' said Monica. 'You could taste the ghost drink, couldn't you? And anyway, surely you don't want to risk it?' She took a step forward. More of the ceiling collapsed right in front of her—but she didn't flinch. 'Come on, Helena,' she said.

Imogen took a step forward too.

'She might prefer to stay with us,' she said. 'We'll be a complete theatre company then. Otherwise, Stoney Vale will always be missing.' Her voice rang out confidently into the dying hall.

'But that's the nature of the character,' said Monica. 'She goes missing in the play.'

Imogen turned round to Helena then.

Helena was kneeling on the floor, her head in her hands.

'You liked being Stoney Vale, didn't you?' said Imogen.

'Yes.'

'Would you want to be her for ever and ever?'

Helena started to say 'yes'—but then stopped in mid-syllable. She wasn't sure.

'I've always wanted to be an actress,' she said. 'I want to play other parts . . . '

'But you'll never get another part as good as Stoney Vale,' said Imogen swiftly.

This silenced Helena. She thought it might be true.

'You may as well be Stoney Vale for ever . . . '

The door-wedge gave out, causing the door to slam shut. There were cracks running all the way up it and across it.

Monica was just in front of it and Imogen was opposite her. All the rest of the theatre company seemed to have faded into the background—in fact, the more Helena tried to look at them, the more they seemed to be actually physically fading—not just metaphorically. She wondered if she was fading herself, it certainly felt like it. The only clear, sharp figures were Monica and Imogen.

'Why do you begrudge Helena her life?' asked Monica. 'It's not her fault you didn't grow up. It's not her fault you lost Michael Green.'

At the mention of that name, Imogen winced as if the memory were painful.

'Helena's not in love with anyone,' she said defiantly. 'She said so. And she doesn't get on with her mother. The best thing she ever did was be Stoney Vale.'

Helena suddenly realized she was holding a fold of her dress in her hands—the green dress her mother had made her. She stood up, causing both Imogen and Monica to turn and stare fixedly at her.

She felt the dress fall softly into place. Her favourite colour was green. Green was supposedly the colour of the sea serpent. Monica's serpent.

'My mum's all right,' she said uncertainly. 'She made this dress for me.'

At this, Monica saw her chance.

'Leave now, Helena,' she said—and took her arm. 'Come on.'

Helena allowed herself to be led forward a few paces. But then she felt a pull on her other arm. Imogen was holding her back and Imogen was very strong. The look in her eyes was terrifying. That alone could have made Helena stay.

'For God's sake, Imogen!' shouted Monica. 'Is this to be a tug of war?'

With one hand, she thrust open the door of the hall.

And then all three of them nearly jumped out of their skins because Trevor was standing there! Trevor—in his pyjamas, looking bemused and distant as if he had been sleep-walking and ended up there.

Suddenly, Helena came violently to her senses.

'Trevor!' she cried in horror. 'What are you doing here? It isn't safe!'

She wrenched herself free of Imogen's grip—but not of Monica's.

'Oh thank God, you're seeing sense,' said Monica.

'No, I'm just seeing my Trevor,' said Helena simply and rushed forward. She pushed Trevor away from the door and didn't stop moving until both of them were clear away from the hall. Only then did she realize that Monica was no longer hanging on to her arm. Still holding Trevor firmly, she spun round to look. Then she was aware of Imogen wildly sobbing and Monica trying to comfort her. Both of them were still standing just inside the hall.

'Monica!' cried Helena—and it came out in a hoarse croak. 'Get out of there!'

The next thing she knew was the whole hall collapsing.

Chapter Nineteen

Aftermath

Helena closed her eyes in horror and screamed but no sound came out of her mouth—like in a nightmare. She was shaking all over but chastising herself too.

'You've got to look, you've got to see, you've got to help Monica . . . '

She made herself open her eyes again and then there was a further shock: there was no sign of the building at all now—collapsed or otherwise.

'Oh my God!' she cried—but then of course it was a ghost hall.

But what of Monica?

She shuddered, expecting she would have to face a broken body. There would just be Monica's—nobody else's. Everyone else was a ghost already.

Her heart was beating so fast, she wondered if she was going to die herself. She turned to deal with Trevor first.

He was now lying curled up on the ground, his head pillowed on his hand and his eyes closed. She was convinced he had been sleep-walking.

Should he be lying on the damp ground, she thought—and realized in a flash how ridiculously trivial that was compared to the state that Monica might be in. And anyway, it wasn't damp. It was a warm summer evening.

Dreadful that such an evening should be so full of horror.

She thought it was safe to leave Trevor for a few minutes. What could happen to him?

Feeling faint and giddy, she forced her feet to move. The

nearer she got to where the hall had been, the more she thought the horrible suspense would kill her.

There would be a mangled body lying in the space.

But there wasn't.

Helena looked wildly around. Had Monica escaped from the hall after all?

But where was she?

Surely she wouldn't have just gone?

Helena found her voice again:

'Monica, Monica!' she screamed and ran into the woods nearest where the hall had been.

No one there.

She started to make off in another direction—and then saw something.

She stood dead still.

Through the shimmering haze of the summer evening, she saw the whole of the Serpenton and High Hat Amateur Theatrical Company. They were walking peacefully down the hill—almost sauntering.

Henry Mead was in front, twirling his trilby on the end of one finger.

She recognized Solly, but only just—because he was out of his pieman costume at last.

The 'lovers' were there, the forty-five-year-old man holding hands with the twenty-eight-year-old woman. Maybe they had become lovers in real life too.

Real life! What was she on about? They were dead.

Dorothy and Miss Smith were chatting as they strolled. Miss Smith was actually swinging her leather case as if she had some life in her at last.

Life! There I go again, thought Helena. It wasn't life, it was death. And never had she felt more left-out and more envious.

The four girls were at the back in their flowery dresses: Imogen, Julia, Meggy, and herself.

What?

For one joyful moment, Helena thought she had died herself and hadn't realized.

But then the girl turned round.

She looked a bit like Helena. There was no doubt about that. Her hair was brown, her eyes were almond-shaped and she had a green dress on. But this dress was a funny length and a different fabric to Helena's. It was more like the dresses the other girls wore.

It's Monica, thought Helena. She's gone back to how she was when it all happened the first time. Fifty years ago. She went with them in the end, not me.

The fourteen-year-old Monica smiled and waved her hand.

Helena waved back but didn't manage to smile.

Nobody else turned round.

Then, as she watched, they faded into the warm green hill and she could see them no more.

She made her way doggedly back to where Trevor was sleeping. She lifted him, put him over her shoulder and started the descent of the hill. A grasshopper chirped somewhere.

She had made her choice: she was staying with the living, not leaving with the ghosts, and all she felt was complete and utter loss.

CHAPTER TWENTY

The Sea Serpent?

Robin and Christine Melling never knew that Trevor had been sleep-walking. Helena decided against telling them. She would just have to hope that he never did it again.

It was quite a feat what he had done: he had left his bedroom, gone downstairs, opened the front door, slipped through it—ironically like a little ghost—closed it behind him and all without his parents knowing. Then he had stealthily made his way through the village and up the High Hat hill.

Helena could see that the alarming phrase 'It Was Meant To Happen' was relevant here—which was how she justified not telling his parents. However, fond as she now was of Trevor, the choice to stay with the living was only painful at the moment. She ached with loss. And particularly for Monica.

The Mellings had heard someone in the village had died, but they had never known Monica and knew nothing of either Helena's or Trevor's involvement.

Just like Stoney Vale's in the play, Monica's body was never found. Mrs Fields told Helena that and she said it completely dead-pan as if no one in the village was surprised. She also handed Helena the green and gold scrap-book that Trevor had done his designs in.

'Monica gave me this yesterday morning to look at,' she said. 'I think you should have it now.'

Helena, who had never seen inside it, took it eagerly. But she didn't open it just yet.

The village was very different now. It was so bright!

There was no suggestion of mist or haze now. Everything stood out clear and sharp. Red geraniums had mysteriously appeared in Monica's window-box—except 'mysteriously' was probably the wrong word now. Nothing could be mysterious in Serpenton any more. The past was played out. Somehow, the window-box looked less odd now.

Helena had to turn away from Monica's house. She brushed the back of her hand across her eyes and walked down to the sea.

The pub was crammed—and the sun streaming into the room.

The beach was so yellow and positive that Helena gasped. She was looking at yards and yards of festive, sparkling sand—and all the shells were whole—not broken into bits. The sea stretched gently over and over—bluer than ink.

It couldn't stay like this always, thought Helena. It's too perfect. Maybe it's terribly negative of me, but didn't I somehow—almost . . . prefer it when it was grey and green and sulky . . . no, no, how could you think like that? How could you?

She walked over to the rocky shingle, sat down, took her shoes off and dangled her bare feet in the perfect sea.

'Where are you, sea serpent?' she said sadly. 'Do you exist? Or not? You did for Monica. Maybe you could for me?'

But the water merely folded itself neatly in front of her.

'They've all gone, sea serpent,' she said. 'They've all gone.'

Then she thought about Trevor's scrap-book. It lay on a rock, all hopeful and jewel-like, while she was miserable. She opened it and turned through the pages, gasping in astonishment and delight. The most exquisite sea serpents were gyrating in front of her—in pencil, seaweed, and newspaper.

'Trust you, Trevor,' she said—then something made her look closely at the newspaper. There was part of a date caught in a sea serpent's neck. It was old newspaper, brought by Monica in the leather satchel—and the date was nineteen forty something.

Helena closed the book reverently and felt a sudden urge to step into the sea.

But the water reached up and stained the bottom of her dress and, for some reason, this brought her back to reality. Mum will kill me if I ruin this, she thought.

And then she had an overwhelming desire to see her. Monica had gone. Maybe she could be friends with another 'older' woman. Maybe it could be her mother . . .

She was wearing green cycling shorts under the dress and nothing else. After a quick look round to check no one else was on the beach, she pulled the dress over her head, left it lying on the rocks next to the scrap-book and plunged deeper into the sea.

She stretched her arms out and arched her back. The water was round her knees now. Something had unsettled it slightly—and made it wilder and saltier. The smell of it was stronger. Seagulls crowded in overhead and their calling made Helena's heart ache and leap—like the day she first arrived there, only with a difference.

Maybe she had 'love' to come. Like Imogen Mead and Michael Green. But maybe she would have it for longer than they did. Hopefully, she was going to be an actress. All sorts of things happened to actresses . . .

Helena laughed for the first time since Monica's death and felt the sun hot on her bare back.

'Helena,' said a sudden voice behind her, sounding rather shocked. 'What are you doing?'

'Hello, James!' she said, without turning round. 'Have you come to take me home?'

She walked backwards through the water, grabbed the dress, pulled it back on and turned to face her brother.

'I came down for the day again,' he said, looking puzzled. 'I thought I'd surprise you.'

'You did,' she said. 'And now you've done that, let's go home.'

'But what about the Mellings and—?'

She interrupted him.

'I'll say goodbye to them first, of course,' she said—and grinned when she thought about showing Trevor's scrapbook to his parents. As far as she could gather, they had nothing at all to show for their arty holiday. But he had. She would always stay in touch with Trevor.

'But there's nothing left for me to do here now,' she said to James.

'What?'

'There isn't,' she assured him. 'I've already done it.'